Dedication

To my vivacious sister,
Emmy Schretter,
whose life was cut short at age 23.

Wilderness Journey

A TRUE LOVE STORY

ERNA M. HOLYER

REVIEW AND HERALD® PUBLISHING ASSOCIATION
HAGERSTOWN, MD 21740

The author assumes full responsibility for the accuracy of
all facts and quotations as cited in this book.

This book was
Edited by Jeannette R. Johnson
Designed by DeLaine Heinlein-Mayden
Cover art by Joel Spector
Typeset: 12/13 Optima

PRINTED IN U.S.A.

01 00 99 98 97   5 4 3 2 1

R&H Cataloging Service
Holyer, Erna Marie, 1925-
    Wilderness journey.

        Series: Vienna Brooks Saga.

    I. Title.   II. Series: Vienna Brooks Saga.

            813.54

ISBN 0-8280-0947-3

Contents

Introduction

The heroine of this book is a real person. Born in 1839 in St. Joseph County, Michigan, to Eliza Ann and George W. Brooks, Vienna was the firstborn of six children and the only girl.

She was the apple of her father's eye and couldn't imagine life without him. Then one day, when Vienna was 11 years old, her father up and left. Vienna was devastated. Her feelings about her father were confused when he—two years later—asked the family to follow him to California.

Vienna's resentment against her father balloons as she experiences the dangers and hardships of the journey. Her strong negative feelings nearly destroy her.

Happily, she meets John, a golden young man who keeps coming to her rescue. She falls in love with him, and he asks her to marry him someday in California.

A clash develops with Mother, who says Vienna is too young and tells John to come back in two or three years. She might as well have said "a lifetime," as far as Vienna is concerned. How she solves her problems is detailed in this book. Though the story happened in 1852, it is of significance to today's young readers. With fathers leaving the family fold and young girls falling in love—and meeting parental resistance—many young readers can identify with the heroine's dilemma.

The experiences of the Brooks family during their epic journey have deeply moved me. I feel that teenaged Vienna must have had the most difficult time because of her added growing-up challenges.

Much of the material for this book is derived from published and unpublished reminiscences of her brother, Elisha Brooks, the family's young teamster on the westward trek. Manuscripts, speeches given in the San Francisco Bay area, articles published in the *Pacific School and Home Journal,* and his booklet, *A Pioneer Mother of California,* all furnished valuable insight.

I wish to thank Mr. Brooks S. Whitney, grandnephew of Vienna Brooks, for the use of these materials.

Erna M. Holyer
San Jose, California

Vienna's mother, Eliza Ann Brooks

Chapter One
Destination California

The shake cabin in the Michigan backwoods tucked under the pines that sighed in the cold April wind. Inside, young Vienna Brooks put away her good dress after coming home from church. Fingering the handmade lace collar, she shrugged off strange forebodings. She wouldn't wear the dress again until the journey to California lay behind her. She looked up, meeting Mother's gaze.

"What if we don't make it, Mother?" she asked, trying to keep the quiver out of her voice.

Mother stroked the girl's thick brown hair, silky beneath her touch despite the callouses hard work had put on Mother's hands. Her brown eyes looked calm in the oval face framed by smooth, center-parted hair. "God will lead us to our new home before winter snows close mountain passes in the Sierra Nevada. God will be with us." Mother's voice was gentle, but firm.

Vienna asked no more questions. The last thing she wanted was for Mother to worry about her only girl. Mother had enough worries already.

Four days later Mother loaded all their possessions—including a stock of provisions and a camp outfit—into the family's new canvas-covered wagon. With the help of the 11-year-old twins, Elisha and Elijah, she yoked eight oxen and hitched the draft animals to the wagon. Vienna fastened two milk cows behind the wagon and tied a coop containing two loudly protesting chickens to the wagon's tail end.

Mounting the high wagon box, they bade goodbye to their old cabin home with its surrounding pines and swamp lands. Dark clouds moved above the swaying treetops and the air smelled of rain. The wind roared high in the pines, and the rushing sound reverberated in Vienna's ears. As they passed their neighbors' log cabins at a distance, Vienna saw a red-haired girl flying down the dirt road.

"Priscilla!" She scrambled from the wagon. Lifting her skirts, she ran toward her friend. The girls embraced in desperation, even though they'd already said their goodbyes after the Sabbath service.

"I had to see you," Priscilla gasped, coppery freckles blushing her face. "You must write about everything that happens on the trail, you hear?"

Vienna noticed tears in her friend's green eyes. She blinked away a few tears of her own.

"You must tell me about all the young gentlemen you meet, you hear?"

Vienna burst out laughing. "I'm 13 years old. I doubt any gentlemen will notice me."

"Oh, but they will! You're pretty, like your ma. Why, you're big enough to be betrothed."

"With five younger brothers to look after, a girl had better do her chores," Vienna said, but she felt flattered. She liked nothing better than being compared to her mother, the tall and slim-waisted Eliza Ann Brooks.

"My ma says she'd feel awful if Pa up and left like yours did," Priscilla prattled. "Pa does all the work around the farm, he and Phil. Ma doesn't have to worry about a thing. She'd never go West without Pa."

"My mother has as much spunk as your pa and she's smart," Vienna retorted. "She has what it takes to get us to California."

Priscilla drew back. "Sure, sure. You're lucky your pa is off. Mine can get so mad when he catches me fussing with my hair."

"He doesn't beat you, does he?"

"No, but he beats Phil."

Vienna frowned. "I'll see my father again in four or five months."

Priscilla's nose wrinkled. "Guess you're not too crazy 'bout meetin' up with your pa, huh?"

"Why do you say that?"

"It's 'cause of him you're in the fix you're in."

Vienna hunched up her shoulders. Her friend's remark stung. "You got it all wrong, Priscilla. My father is staking out a future for us in the Far West. The sawmill he and other Michigan lumbermen built has a summer's worth of cut wood near the *Rio de las Plumas*— that's Feather River in English. There's a fortune to be made in lumber. Miners are washing big nuggets from the streams; they pay for boards with *gold*. You can stay in these backwoods if you like; I'm going to California!"

Priscilla's face darkened. "Why, if that's the way you feel, then don't even bother to write!" She ran off, red braids bouncing on frail shoulders.

"What was that all about?" Mother asked from the wagon.

"Oh, nothing!" Vienna grappled with her feelings. Why had Priscilla's remarks unsettled her? Why had she allowed herself to fly off the handle? She felt confused and hurt.

Two weeks had passed since Father's long-awaited letter arrived from the gold mines. In 1850 (when she was going on 12) Father had caught the raging gold fever. Vienna remembered it well . . .

Bearded men galloping to the cabin on brown horses.

13

Rough voices asking for Father. The men had drummed up a party destined for California. They pestered Father, threatened, cajoled.

"The streets are paved with gold in California," they promised. "Californios live 150 years in perfect health. If you stay here, George Washington Brooks, the ague will kill you or the fever will do you in. You look like a ghost already, man. You've gotta hurry afore the land is taken and the gold runs out. Come with us now and send for the family later."

The men wore down Father's resistance. He listened to them like Samson had listened to the wicked Delilah.

He'd make a home for his family, Father's letter explained. It was a promise Mother couldn't ignore. She'd do anything to reunite the family. Vienna marveled at the speed and zest with which Mother had arranged for the overland journey. A man couldn't have shown more foresight. From blacksmith to cartwright to outfitting store, she kept everybody busy, demonstrating amazing organizational skills.

All the family lacked was a teamster to handle the eight oxen, and a wagon train to join for safety.

"God will provide," Mother answered Vienna's unspoken question. She countered the girl's silence with her searching, direct look.

Elisha, the bolder of the twins, took the reins from her hand. "Let me drive, Mother!" The boy cracked the whip. The long-horned oxen strained in their yokes and the wheels turned in the soft ground.

"Hurrah!" Elisha's dark-haired twin, Elijah, and the three blond boys, 9-year-old Justus, 6-year-old Orion, and 4-year-old Elmont, cheered, faces aglow with excitement.

Vienna thought she'd never get used to the wagon's rocking. Fat tears stained the diary she held on her lap. She wiped them away with the crisp hem of her pinafore.

Left St. Joseph County, Michigan, on April 28, 1852.

She stared at the penciled entry. The date represented a turning point in her life. Her childhood friend, the adored schoolmaster, and the respected Elder—no longer would she see their beloved faces. Nor would she warm herself in the cozy log cabin her parents had built as newlyweds.

"A wagon train! Look!"

The twin's cry jolted Vienna. It was true; Elisha's eagle eye had spotted billowing canvas tops.

"The rumors we heard at the parish were true," Vienna stated. She felt hugely relieved knowing they'd soon travel in company.

A wagon train was forming at the nearby lumbering village. They found the leader, who advised Mother to engage a driver in exchange for passage.

"Can you recommend somebody?" Mother asked.

"Reckon so, ma'am." The bearded man bridled his horse. "A certain Jeffrey came around this morning. Carried himself well. The lad's rarin' to travel."

"Thank you most kindly, sir. We shall look for the lad in camp." Mother climbed down from the wagon, leaving Vienna in charge. She returned with a beardless, fair-skinned lumberman, who carried his bundle on square shoulders. Jolly eyes danced under his home-styled haircut as he respectfully introduced himself to Vienna.

"Why are you going west, Jeffrey?" Vienna liked the well-scrubbed lad. He couldn't be more than 17, she guessed.

"Michigan's swamps aren't very healthy, ma'am." Jeffrey helped Mother into the wagon, then tossed up his bundle.

Vienna giggled and moved over. Nobody had ever called her "ma'am" before.

"I hear they have much sunshine in the Far West," Jeffrey continued, taking his seat beside the girl. "A dry climate isn't likely to give a man the fever." He took whip and reins and directed the oxen to fall in line with the other teams.

Clouds threatened rain and the emigrants desired to

leave. Since the train was large enough, the leader decided they should pull out and use the remaining daylight hours for traveling.

The wagons rumbled past the lumbering village to the sound of cheers, prayers, and hymns of settlers who came out to see them off. Women wept on seeing the children on the wagons. One kind-hearted lady handed up cold biscuits. Mother accepted the gifts, visibly moved.

"Bless you, sister."

Vienna's eyes swam. "Bless you," she added.

The first drops began to fall, and soon rain came down in sheets. Mother herded the boys under the canvas roof and beckoned Vienna to take shelter. Vienna hated to leave Jeffrey. The young driver sat hunched over, keeping the oxen in line.

"Go on inside, ma'am," he encouraged.

Vienna ducked under the canvas. Rain prattled down, softening the road and taxing the animals. The family huddled uncomfortably between barrels, trunks, rolled-up blankets, and a sheet-iron stove.

Even so, Mother appeared pleased. "We are on our way, children." She enunciated every word in her crisp style. "The new oxen are uncoordinated, but Jeffrey is handling them well."

"I'll help Jeffrey," Elisha offered. "I know how to handle Nig and Brock."

Mother tousled the twin's darkening hair. "Your darling pets are doing the most important job in front of the wheel. I am glad you and Elijah trained our wheelers."

Vienna was happy when the wagons ascended a rise, spread out between the broken stands of pine, and drivers unhitched the oxen. About to jump into the wet grass with the milk pail, she caught Jeffrey's eye. He was securing the oxen with long ropes to keep them from straying.

"Allow me, ma'am!" He took the pail from her hand, then put the milking stool under a cow. The steady stream

Journey

of milk swishing into the pail and the soothing words he spoke to relax the cow told Vienna that Jeffrey was an expert milker.

Smiling, she filled his tin cup with the frothy, cow-warm milk before he released the cows to graze.

"Thank you most kindly, ma'am." He returned the cup with a smile, then marched off through the rain. Returning with an armload of pine branches, he joked about the "pioneers' mattresses." However, his barely-started campfire vanished in thin clouds of smoke.

"Doused!" He grinned up at Vienna.

Justus, the blond 9-year-old, added a childish joke, and soon the entire family was laughing.

Mother heated soup and the kind lady's biscuits in the sheet-iron stove. They ate, huddling together under the canvas. Jeffrey and the twins erected two small tents; they'd sleep outside. Then the moment Vienna had been dreading arrived. She crawled under the dripping wagon with Mother. Behind a shield of blankets, she got her first taste of camping out.

The lusty cackling of a laying hen roused her at dawn. Her clothes felt damp; her teeth chattered. Mother stirred beside her. She offered a cheerful good morning.

"This is going to be a good day, daughter. We shall use the egg for breakfast." Mother's voice rang clear as a bell.

Vienna peeked out through the wheel spokes. Jeffrey was up. He had taken down his tent and finished untangling the oxens' ropes.

"How was bivouacking under the wagon, ma'am?" he asked.

"Fine, thanks to your pine branches." If others could show spirit so could she, Vienna decided. Putting starch into her spine, she climbed up with as much dignity as her stiff limbs allowed.

Jeffrey tied the cows behind the wagon, then came for the milk pail as if he were one of the family. Vienna re-

Wilderness Journey

17

joiced. She'd always wished for an older brother. Warm milk and hot flapjacks made a wonderful breakfast. Even Justus and Elijah, the fussy eaters, ate with gusto.

The camp sprang alive with the bellowing of cows and oxen, the crack of ox-goads, and drivers' resounding "whoa-haws." The yoking and hitching of the draft animals took place under a great bustle of confusion. The wagons finally descended to the muddy road and fell in line. Rain came down in torrents, drenching drivers and animals alike. Vienna put a dry blanket over Jeffrey, who thanked her with a happy smile.

The wagons were strung out. Some sank into soft depressions, while others rounded knolls to avoid getting stuck. Temperatures dropped by midday, and the rain turned into blinding snow. The blizzard over, Vienna peeked out at a wintry scene and glimpses of the solemn St. Joseph River.

"Whoa!" Jeffrey set the brake.

Mother quit rocking the rosy-faced Elmont. "Is anything wrong, Jeffrey?"

"Our lead wagon seems to be stuck, ma'am." He jumped down and sloshed to the front. The men bridged a slough with freshly gathered brush and got the wagons moving. The train managed three more crossings before pitching camp for the night.

Vienna spent the night shivering under the wagon. She huddled close to Mother while the ground froze and the pine branch mattress got colder by the hour. She yearned for a crackling fire.

"Why do we have to travel in snow and rain, when our cabin back home is dry and warm?" she muttered.

She worried about the news they'd heard during the day—that several children had come down with fever. She worried about Elisha, whose groans sounded from the twins' tent. The boy had been in some sort of pain all day.

Chapter Two
Broken Sabbath

The peculiar noises of cows ripping half-frozen grass from the ground woke Vienna at dawn. She strained to hear any faint moaning sounds that might be coming from Elisha's tent. She felt too cold to check on her brother or on the younger boys, who curled up in the wagon box like a litter of pups. Mother slept peacefully. Grateful for the warmth from her body, Vienna didn't wake her.

She dozed until teamsters' shouts disrupted the morning stillness. Smoke and cooking odors drifted into her nostrils. She stirred. Her breath puffed in white clouds as she slipped through the blankets fastened around the wheels. Dark clouds gathered overhead and treetops sighed like tired old men. Shivering in her wool shawl, she lifted the twins' tent flap and peered inside. Even breathing told her the boys were asleep. She didn't rouse them, but checked on her little brothers in the wagon.

"Mama! Where's Mama?" Little Elmont stuck his cherub head out of the blankets.

"Hush. She'll be right up." Vienna busied herself at the stove. By the time Mother climbed up and Jeffrey asked for the milk pail, she had a fire going.

The twins emerged from their tent. Elisha looked miserable, but it was his twin who warmed himself by the stove. The twins looked alike, taking after Mother and resembling Vienna with their brown-haired good looks. Subtle differences distinguished them. Comfort came first with Elijah. He was the twin who changed his mind about right and wrong. Elisha, though impulsive and daring, could definitely tell the difference.

Mother touched his forehead. "So what is ailing this young man?"

"N-nothing," Elisha stammered.

"A tummy ache?"

"Uh-huh."

"What did you eat?"

"N-nothing."

"We must not lie, young man!" Mother checked supplies. She pulled a sack from a barrel and held it up. "Did you get into our dried apple slices, Elisha?"

"I, uh, am sorry, Mother. I won't do it again, I promise! I'm sorry I lied—and stole."

Mother's eyes grew stern. "Our supplies are meant to last, children. Times will come when we shall desperately need our food to survive. Out in the wilderness we may not find any towns, shops, or merchants. If we waste food now, what shall we eat in the wilderness?"

The 11-year-old covered his face. "I hadn't thought of that, Mother. I deserve to be punished so I remember good and well."

Mother turned to Vienna. "What shall be your brother's punishment, daughter?"

Vienna suppressed her sudden mirth. "Elisha suffered all night, Mother. He has been punished already. He's learned his lesson, don't you think?" She felt like laughing aloud. Dried apples indeed! Elisha got off with an admonition, and she still felt like laughing when Jeffrey brought the milk.

"What's so funny?" He looked surprised.

"Oh, Jeffrey, I thought Elisha was dying. I thought we'd all die from some terrible fever only because my brother ate dried apples." She threw back her head and laughed. And suddenly the entire family was laughing with her. Hot cornbread tasted wonderful, and the first part of the day's drive was fun.

Road and weather conditions wiped the smiles off their faces. Sloughs had to be bridged and crossed. Every able-bodied person—man, woman, and child—walked in order to lighten the load. While Jeffrey helped cut small trees, Vienna and the boys carried willow branches. She braced herself against the wind as icy needles of sleet stung her face.

All jesting stopped as the bundled-up emigrants coaxed the teams onto makeshift bridges and kept the wagon wheels from sinking out of sight. A blizzard piled snow on wagons and draft animals after the second crossing, and the road disappeared, much to Jeffrey's dismay.

"I'm glad I'm not driving the lead wagon," he told Vienna. The wagon in front of them vanished from view and the oxen moved like ghosts in the white blur.

"How do you know where we're going?" Vienna clicked her feet together in an effort to keep them warm.

"I listen to the other drivers' commands." Jeffrey's words sounded muted. He resembled a shapeless snowman under the tent material he had draped around himself.

"Don't you wish you'd stayed home? I really miss our old log cabin." Vienna glanced at Jeffrey.

"Who, me? Stay home? Only softies stay home."

"My friend Priscilla is staying home," Vienna volunteered. "Her mother said *she* wouldn't go West without her husband. Does this make her a softie?"

"Sure sounds like it to me." Jeffrey swung the rawhide whip over his head, then forward again, to let it pop over the oxens' ears. "What's your friend like? Is she pretty?"

"She's my age, but she's short. She has red hair and

green eyes, and when she gets mad her eyes turn dark and her freckles run together."

"What does she get mad about?"

"The last time she got mad at me was because—" Vienna didn't finish. Priscilla's remarks still hurt.

Jeffrey looked at her sharply. "What did you say she got mad about?"

Heat rose to Vienna's face. "I don't want to talk about it. Forget what I said."

"You brought it up," Jeffrey flared. "Just don't start things if you can't finish them." He slapped the snow from his lap, looking grim.

Vienna wished she hadn't mentioned Priscilla. She suppressed a yawn. Hugely tired, she stuck her head into the wagon. "Can we change places, Mother? I'm cold."

She slipped into the wagon as Mother took her seat. Chin dropping on her chest, she clambered over barrels and bedrolls and wedged herself into the boys' bed.

"A village! There's a village ahead!" Jeffrey's cry roused her. Not wanting to move, she saw that Orion, her special charge, had snuggled up.

"Where are we, Orion?"

"Across the river."

"The river! You mean I slept through the crossing?" She struggled out of the blankets. Elijah, Justus, and little Elmont perched in the rear of the wagon, peeking out and reporting on what they saw.

"Don't leave," 6-year-old Orion pleaded.

Vienna stroked his soft blond hair. Orion was a friendly boy, independent as a rule, but clinging of late. "I'll be right back."

She draped the wool shawl around her shoulders, shivering. Icy air pricked her nostrils as she parted the canvas. A glance over Jeffrey's shoulder revealed that the snowstorm had stopped. Log cabins rambled alongside the road, and chimneys sent out sweet-smelling hickory smoke.

Vienna sniffed with pleasure. Dogs barked and people ran out of the houses.

Mother was marching beside the wagon. She waved, looking cold but cheerful. "The good people from the village are coming to greet us, daughter."

Vienna wondered why so few emigrants left the train to greet the settlers. Where was everybody? Elisha was running toward a heavy-set woman. They talked, then both grinned. He came running back with the puffing woman in tow.

"Mother! Vienna! I can sleep by the fireplace!" He shouted, brown eyes snapping.

The woman followed Elisha to the rear of the wagon, then clapped her fat hands together at the sight of the little boys.

"Your sons are welcome to sleep with mine tonight," she told Mother. "Hot mush and a blazing fire will thaw them out."

"May the Lord bless you, sister." Mother climbed up into the wagon and handed down the bundled-up boys.

The train encamped near the village. Too frozen to

> **Corn meal Mush**
>
> The woman clapped her hands together at the sight of the little boys. "Your sons are welcome to sleep with mine tonight," she told Mother. "Hot mush and a blazing fire will thaw them out."
>
> 1 teaspoon salt
> 1 cup stoneground yellow cornmeal
>
> Bring 4 cups of water to a boil in a kettle, and stir in salt. Put the meal in a bowl so you can gather it up easily in your hand. Using one hand to stir the water with a spoon, sprinkle in the meal with the other hand. When all the meal has been stirred in, reduce heat and simmer for at least 1 hour, stirring every 10 minutes to prevent burning and to test thickness. The mush is done when it looks like cooked oatmeal. (6 small servings) Eat cold or hot, with milk or with butter and syrup or sugar.

make a fire, Vienna supped on cold biscuits and cow-warm milk. She shared the cramped wagon box with Mother. Jeffrey made his bed under the wagon, saving himself the bother of putting up his tent. Mother spoke a special prayer of thanks for the boys' warm sleeping quarters.

"This will be a fine Sabbath day, daughter," Mother said. "We can attend Divine Services in the village."

Sabbath? Vienna had lost track of time. Everything, including time, seemed distorted since leaving home. She fell asleep with visions of kneeling in a warm place.

A trumpet blast roused the camp before sunrise. The captain rode from wagon to wagon, ordering the emigrants to leave posthaste. Mother objected.

"We must stay and rest," she said. "Have you forgotten that this is the Sabbath?"

The captain held his horse in check. "We should be glad to stay, ma'am. However, the settlers are telling us to leave lest their families catch our chills and fevers."

Mother stood her ground. "My children and I shall rest and pray. We are well."

"If you stay, you'll fall behind ma'am. We cannot wait for stragglers," the captain warned.

"We shan't move." Mother turned to Jeffrey, who stood idle. "We can make speed tomorrow, can't we, Jeffrey?"

The young teamster paled. "There are bad sloughs to be crossed, ma'am. It takes strong men to get teams and wagons across. We cannot manage by ourselves."

The captain tipped his hat. "The lad is right, ma'am. Better make up your mind soon, for we're pulling out early." With that, he dashed to the next wagon.

"We shan't move." Mother climbed into the wagon and started a fire in the sheet-iron stove. Jeffrey unhappily asked for the milk pail, and Vienna collected the warm egg a loudly cackling hen deposited in the coop.

"I'll take over from here, Mother, so you can fetch the boys," she offered.

"Bless you, daughter." Mother tucked a wisp of hair into her bonnet before leaving. Her brown eyes held a steely gleam.

Jeffrey waited with the milk. "We must talk sense into Mrs. Brooks," he stressed. "There's no way we can catch up with the train tomorrow."

Vienna stirred batter. The damp weather had made the flour lumpy. "God rested on the seventh day and so must we, Jeffrey."

"Well, I'm leaving with the train! Somebody else will give me passage."

Vienna was shocked. "Why, Jeffrey! You cannot leave us. You're like one of the family, and we need you."

"I'm going West, and I'm going now!" Jeffrey's hair fell over stormy brows.

"A day's delay won't hurt, Jeffrey."

"It will if we fall behind. Every day counts. Haven't you heard of the Donner Party? They took a fearful end in the high Sierra." He shook himself, looking disgusted. "They say the mountain passes fill up with snow as high as trees. Woe to the emigrant who gets there too late in the year! The Donner Party was too late, and they paid for it."

"Oh, Jeffrey, where's your faith? I'm disappointed in you." Vienna turned her back to the teamster. While busying herself by the stove, she pretended not to care.

He jumped from the wagon and noisily gathered his things.

"He's going to leave us," Vienna muttered. She blinked back stinging tears.

Mother brought the boys, looking distraught. "It is true what the captain said, daughter. The settlers insist on our departure."

Mother and Vienna breakfasted in silence. Jeffrey ate outside. His bundle lay on the wagon seat.

Drivers' commands punctuated the air. Shouts and whip crackings sounded up front. Oxen lurched forward, and the train began to move. Drivers behind the Brookses wagon made a wide birth around the roped oxen and closed up rank.

"Is anything broken?" they yelled.

"Nothing is broken. I'll see you shortly," Jeffrey yelled back. Turning to Mother, he asked, "Do you want me to yoke the oxen, or not? If you don't, I shall take my leave now."

Mother stood tall. "Sorry, Jeffrey. It is the Sabbath."

Vienna shaded her eyes against rare sun rays breaking through the clouds. Three armed men were approaching on foot.

"Why aren't these oxen yoked?" they charged Jeffrey.

"Go ask her." Jeffrey stabbed a thumb at Mother high on the wagon.

Mother confronted the men with composure. "We shan't travel today."

The tallest man waved his rifle at the twins, whose dark heads popped out of the foremost hoop.

"Two of our children came down with a fever last night," he accused. "The babes were healthy until you people arrived, and now they may die. You do us no favor by staying here."

Mother put her arms around the twins. "We wish your children no harm."

"Prove it! Do a good deed on the Sabbath and take yourselves out of here." The tall man fingered his rifle.

Mother looked ill. Vienna guessed she was grappling with a decision. The captain arrived on his steaming horse. He shot a sidelong glance at the settlers' rifles, then spoke to Mother in even tones.

"Consider your family's safety, ma'am. You may kill the little ones by staying behind. The westward journey is no child's play. Strong men have perished in the wilderness by going it alone."

Mother's lips trembled. Finally, her shoulders drooped.

"Put the oxen to the wagon, Jeffrey. We are leaving."

Vienna felt sick. This could have been a day of joy! She summoned her brothers. Lacking kneeling room, they stood, chanting their prayers and listening to Mother's quotations from the Bible. Vienna noticed that Mother's hands shook as they held the black Book.

Service over, the family lightened the load by walking. Melting snow glistened on the marshy ground. Vienna's shoes squished, and she felt the clammy dampness. Jeffrey's grumbling added to her discomfort.

"Now we'll forever travel at the rear and swallow dust, and all because a woman couldn't make up her mind."

Vienna shot him a defiant glance. "It will be a while until we see some dust, Jeffrey. If I were you I'd worry more about steering clear of these wagon ruts." Her feeling for Jeffrey had changed. She was glad he wasn't her brother.

The sight of Lake Michigan let her forget the driver's bad mood. A sea of grey water stretched ahead. Wind-whipped waves seemingly rolled on to the ends of the earth. Vienna heard a watery plop of hooves even before the captain's voice rang out.

"We must fill a big slough. We need every able-bodied helper."

Jeffrey set the brake. Mother handed him an axe. "I shall stay in the wagon with my little boys. I shan't work today," she told the teamster.

Elisha, Elijah, and Justus sloshed after Jeffrey. Vienna trudged behind. Following some grown men, they walked a mile to find the brush required to fill the slough. The men cut down small willow trees. Vienna and the boys carried branches to the slough. The sun slipped in and out of the clouds, passing the zenith, and still the willow bridge didn't hold.

The first teams ventured across the makeshift bridge in the afternoon. Vienna dumped branches as two horses struggled in the mire and drowned despite the men's efforts to save them. She noticed that the first wagons made it across.

A seasoned teamster volunteered to drive the Brookses' wagon at the end of the train. Mother helped little Elmont and Orion from the wagon. She watched the crossing, somber-faced.

Vienna's hand flew to her mouth as the oxen sank to their bellies, and the wagon box disappeared in the mud. The wagon was their home. What if they lost it and the supplies it contained? She worried herself sick.

The teamster's persistent goading got the lead oxen to the opposite side. Husky men pulled at the rope fastened to the wagon tongue. Miraculously, the oxen found footing and the wheels reappeared.

The emigrants' cheers notwithstanding, the bridge of brush had slipped beneath the ooze. The last woodcutters brought slender poles and laid them across the two half-submerged horses. Brave lads danced across and waved their hats on the other side. Children crossed without mishap.

Vienna gathered her skirts. The pole felt slippery under her muddy shoes. Heart pounding, she balanced herself across. Keenly aware of a moldy smell, she joined her brothers. Looking back, she saw that Mother was nudging little Elmont to the pole. The 4-year-old clung screaming to Mother's skirt. Other women went ahead. The women uttered anxious little shrieks as they gingerly picked up their skirts, daring the pole. A bearded man lifted Elmont in his arms and attempted to carry the boy across. Elmont kicked and screamed, so the man handed Elmont back to his mother.

Mother set foot onto the pole, carrying the clinging child. Vienna's throat tightened. Mother couldn't see where she was going, not with Elmont in her arms. She walked slowly, deliberately, face devoid of color. In mid-slough, she seemed to falter. She struggled for balance, then slipped and fell, sprawling into the mire.

"Help! Somebody help her!" Vienna screamed. About to dash into the mud, she felt herself restrained by muscled arms.

Chapter Three
Funeral in the Snow

Vienna struggled in vain against the strong arms that held her captive. "Grab the pole, Mother!" she shouted. "Climb on the horse! Hang on!"

Mother and child thrashed in the mire. Mother succeeded in shoving Elmont onto one of the drowned horses. As she attempted to hoist herself onto the carcass, she slipped. Vienna watched horror-stricken as her shoulders disappeared in the ooze.

"Somebody, please jump in and help! We mustn't lose Mother. What would we do without her?" Looking at the bystanders, she screamed, "Please save our mother!"

One of the men tossed Mother a rope and succeeded in pulling the mud-covered woman ashore. The captain extended a board to Elmont and coaxed the boy to crawl out on the wobbly wood.

Kind women led Mother and child to the wagon. Vienna pulled clean clothes from a trunk and handed them to the women. While they fussed over Mother, she rinsed the muddy clothes in the water bucket outside and hoped the next day's sunshine would dry them.

Mother was clutching her youngest after the women

left. "We almost lost our dear little Elmont," she babbled. "What would Father say if we arrived without our baby? Elmont doesn't remember his father. I raised him alone for the last two years."

"You're both safe, Mother," Vienna comforted. "Rest now. You mustn't take a chill."

Mother didn't protest. The company pitched camp near the slough and Vienna cooked supper on the smoking campfire.

A howling storm came up after dark. Rain fell in torrents, soaking bedding and clothing. The slough overflowed, covering the camp with inches of water. Vienna fled her sodden bed under the wagon, and the twins escaped their collapsed tent in the black of night. Soaked to the skin and chattering, the family huddled under the wagon's flapping canvas, only to resume their wet journey in the morning.

"We shan't forget our Slough of Despond," Mother told the children. "It will remind us of our broken Sabbath."

"It wasn't your fault, Mother," Vienna pointed out. "The villagers threatened us at gunpoint."

"Nevertheless, daughter, God did not give us a spirit of timidity."

She didn't mention the slough again, but Vienna recorded the happening in her diary. Chilled to the bone, wearing flannels and an overcoat, she forced herself to make the entry. Her stiff fingers wouldn't close around the lead pencil, making for poor penmanship.

Many wet days and nights later, they spotted a large stream ahead. The twins saw it first.

"A big river! Look!"

The twins' excited cries brought a feeble smile to Mother's face. They crossed the Mississippi on a ferry boat that was large enough to hold wagon and team. Two horses in a treadmill, one on each side, propelled the boat. Mother's hands clamped and unclamped as the ferry took them seven miles up a western branch of the river in search of a landing place. The boys cheered and Mother relaxed when Jeffrey finally drove the oxen safely onto solid ground.

"We're now in Iowa, the 29th state of the Union," Jeffrey boasted. "After Iowa, we'll strike out into the wilderness. Hurrah!"

"What's out there?" Vienna asked. She had established an uneasy truce with the teamster.

"Adventure and a pot of gold at the end of the rainbow." Jeffrey whistled through his teeth. "I'll be a rich man with gold in every pocket! I'll build me a mansion and marry the prettiest girl around."

"You said you're going west for your health," Vienna reminded him.

"That, too."

"Aren't you afraid, Jeffrey? I mean, there won't be anybody to protect us."

"Me—afraid?" Jeffrey scoffed. "Once we leave Iowa we'll be traveling in a large train. We'll have experienced leaders. Indians won't dare attack us with their silly bows and arrows. After all, we have firearms."

"What about other dangers?" Vienna ventured.

"What about them?" Jeffrey shrugged.

Vienna made a new entry in her diary: *Jeffrey is not afraid.* Her next entry, written somewhere in Iowa, stated, *All our boys down with the measles.*

The train stopped for the measles epidemic. Vienna rummaged through the medicine chest, extracting castor oil and peppermint essence. She helped nurse her brothers, while six inches of snow covered the ground and icicles glittered in tree branches.

When two children in the wagons succumbed to the fever, Mother sent Jeffrey to help the men prepare for the funeral. Vienna, mending clothes and boiling tea in the wagon, listened to muted ax blows. A cottonwood tree was being felled to be shaped into small coffins. A stone-cutter worked at chiseling the childrens' names, ages, and date of death into a crude tombstone by the way-side, where the fathers of the deceased youngsters dug a shallow grave.

People well enough to walk joined the funeral procession. The leader offered a prayer at the graveside and the emigrants sang a hymn with much feeling. Mother's hymn-book shook in her hands. Her voice, usually clear as a bell, broke. She wept uncontrollably as two men lowered the small coffins. Vienna was too stunned for tears. During the company's week-long rest, she felt listless and moody. She was lucky this time she figured, for she had weathered the measles before.

The day the train pulled out Vienna looked back at the grave until they disappeared around a bend. Supposing they had left behind her brothers. Supposing Elisha, Elijah, Justus, Orion, or Elmont had died! She got impatient with the twins sometimes, but leaving them behind in a solitary grave? She couldn't bear the thought.

Priscilla popped into her thoughts. She wished she and her childhood friend had parted in peace. She tore a page from her diary and composed a letter.

Priscilla, dear friend,

We shall soon enter the land of the Red Man. Jeffrey, our teamster, is not afraid, and Mother says we'll make it. In case anything happens to me, I want you to know that I am not angry at you anymore. I don't know what came over me. You know it isn't like me to fly off the handle. Can you forgive?

Jeffrey is 17 years old. He calls me ma'am. He says he'll build a mansion in California and marry the pret-tiest girl around. I told him about you.

Mother and the boys join me in wishing you well. Give our love to your parents and Phil.

Your friend, Vienna Brooks.

She wrote in tiny letters to fit her message onto the page. She folded the paper, wrote Priscilla's address up front, then dribbled candle wax on the fold, sealing the letter.

Nearing the Missouri River they saw wagons going east. Rather than striking out into the wilderness, their owners had decided to return to their old homes in the States.

Nearing the high bluffs overlooking the wide bottomland of the Missouri, Vienna flinched at hearing anguished cries.

"Indians! Indians!"

A band of feathered, fringed, wild-maned Indians swooped upon the train on wind-swift horses, barring the way. Vienna scrambled into the wagon and tossed a blanket over her head. Wedged between a bean barrel and the wagon jack, she feared the worst. To her surprise, she heard the captain's muffled call.

"Give them some trinkets, Mrs. Brooks. Beads, calico, or a looking glass. These Indians are friendly Pawnees."

Mother rummaged in a trunk, then handed some things to the jabbering Indians. Vienna stayed under the blanket until the wagon rumbled on. Plucking up courage, she peered out of the foremost hoop. No trace was left of them. Instead, she watched long trains of oxen and billowing wagon tops that moved toward Kanesville, the last outpost of civilization.

The place was teeming with Mormons (Latter Day Saints), waiting to be called to Salt Lake by their leader, Brigham Young, Vienna learned along the way. Thousands of white tents stretched against the high cliffs bordering the prairie. Vienna saw canvas-topped wagons, grazing cattle, makeshift tents, log huts, and even a few frame buildings.

The outfitting town was called Kanesville by some, Council Bluffs by others. The place bustled with activity such as Vienna hadn't seen in all of her nearly 14 years of life. Acrid smoke rose from campfires. Pungent coffee and bacon odors permeated the air. Riders on horses and mules dashed about. People and animals scrambled and jostled.

Cattle bellowed, horses whinnied, mules brayed. Strange dialects and foreign accents created a veritable Babel. Vienna found the scene exciting—and upsetting too.

The Michiganders formed a circle, unyoked their teams, and loosened the milk cows. Young men on horseback drove the bawling cattle away from the overgrazed area. The Brooks company camped between wagon trains coming from many directions.

Vienna shrank from shocking words and crude laughs. She recorded her impresssions. The letter for Priscilla still rested uneasily between the pages of her diary. Jeffrey, who said he'd visit the town, scoffed at her request to post the letter.

After unyoking the oxen and chaining the wagon tongue to the rear wheel of the wagon ahead, he left the milking to Vienna. The twins put up their tent without him and gave the chicken coop a thorough cleaning. Mother cooked, and the younger boys played tag between the wagon wheels. Herders brought back the livestock at dark and closed the wagon circle.

A fiddler struck up a tune around a flickering campfire. Soon lusty voices joined in singing new words to a Stephen Foster melody that had become the theme song of the "forty-niners" and pioneers:

> "I soon shall be in Frisco
> And there I'll look around,
> And when I see the gold lumps there,
> I'll pick them off the ground.
> I'll scrape the mountains clean my boys,
> I'll drain the rivers dry,
> A pocketful of rocks bring home,
> So brothers, don't you cry!"

Then their voices rose almost to a shout on the chorus:

> "Oh Susanna,
> Don't you cry for me!
> I'm going to Cal-i-for-ni-a,
> With my wash pan on my knee!"

Jeffrey finally returned in a bad mood. "I don't like it, don't like it at all," he grumbled while putting up his tent in the light of the dying fire. The next morning he hurried into town.

Vienna entrusted Priscilla's letter to Mother, who took the twins into the outfitting town to purchase supplies. She stayed with the wagon and kept an eye on her little brothers. Justus, Orion, and Elmont were playing under a wagon. Orion was "building a house," his favorite occupation. His brothers were handing him "building materials," sticks mostly. Wash fluttered on lines strung between wagons, youngsters played games in the empty circle, and a baby squalled in a wagon.

Men came and went to have oxen shod and wagon parts repaired. Vienna overheard the men's talk. The town was filled with tales of Indian massacres, starvation, and pestilence. While her knitting needles clicked away, she picked up blood-curdling rumors.

A grimy stranger went from wagon to wagon. He was a bear of a man, burly, and just as shaggy. Was he coming her way? Vienna tensed. The man's hat was pushed back, exposing bushy brows, a coarse red beard, and cruel eyes. Unkempt hair curled over his neck and collar. Coming closer, his blood-shot eyes sized her up.

Vienna put down her knitting. Instinctively, she looked around for help. What was taking Mother so long? Why wasn't Jeffrey back yet? Her brothers were playing several wagons away; she guessed they were safe.

The stranger rocked the wagon tongue, scaring her half to death. He then planted himself beside the girl. Vienna saw that his bulbous nose was red and peeling. Broken veins laced his skin, wriggling over his face like nasty worms.

"W-what do you want?" she asked.

"You alone?" He pulled back the canvas flap and peered into the wagon.

"My brothers are close by, and our teamster's due back

any minute now. Besides, my mother is over there, see?" She vaguely pointed to the next camp.

The stranger drew back. "You wouldn't be kiddin' me, lass?"

She couldn't tell whether he was amused, scared, or angry. Her heart was thrashing. She couldn't bear the man's offensive odor nor the black snuff that ran over his red beard.

"Don't be coy with me, Snappy Eyes! I've a proposition to make."

"W-what kind?" Vienna's knees turned to jelly.

"Your yellow-bellied teamster isn't going to risk his scalp out yonder in Indian country. Takes a real man to ward off them savages."

"W-what do you want?"

"I kin drive you, lass."

"We have a teamster already, and he's not afraid of Indians." Vienna sat up straight. Somewhere in the back of her mind flashed a scripture text. "Be not dismayed, for I am your God; I will strengthen you. I will help you."

"What's your teamster's name?" the stranger demanded.

"Jeffrey."

"Jeff, the milk face?" The stranger's belly laugh made Vienna's flesh crawl. He slapped his thigh. "Came to the fire last night, that one. Was scared as h—"

"Don't finish; I won't have it!" Vienna warned.

"That so?" He swung himself onto the seat beside her. Eyes glittering, he snarled, "Will you have me, or won't you?"

Chapter Four
Panic at Council Bluffs

Go 'way! You have no business here." Vienna was now standing, ready to flee. The bearlike man yanked her arm. It hurt clear to her shoulder. He laughed at the girl's gasp of pain.

"Git in the wagon, lass," he ordered. "Gimme some of that soup I'm smellin'." Still holding her arm, he crawled into the wagon like some creature from the underworld.

"Help! Help!" Vienna yelled at the top of her lungs. She pummeled the man's chest with her free hand. In a surge of panic, she knew he would not let her go.

"Help!" she screeched, hoping against hope somebody might come to her rescue.

"Leave the girl be!" A manly voice cut through the camp's background noises.

And suddenly women came running from every direction. Screaming, swinging sticks of firewood and bundles of wash, they rushed to the girl's aid.

Vienna's attacker swore through his smelly, snuff-smeared beard. Releasing the girl, he fled before the women's weapons. Vienna steadied herself on the wagon.

Beyond the women, she saw the owner of that manly voice. He sat tall on a golden chestnut mare, contemplating her with concern.

"You all right, miss?" he asked.

"I reckon so." Vienna stood under the spell of the rider's sky-blue eyes.

"Thank the Lord!" He soothed his restlessly pacing mare, then set off at a swinging trot.

"Wait! What's your name?" Vienna called after him.

He turned briefly, tipping his hat. "John."

Spellbound, Vienna watched him wend his way between tents and wagons. The women who had chased the evil man into flight gave her no time for reflection.

"Poor child," they commiserated. "Why, you must be scared out of your wits. Did that old lecher hurt you?"

"No, but I am ever so grateful you came. God bless you for your kindness." Vienna rubbed her smarting arm. She could have hugged the women.

"Where is your father?" they wanted to know. "In a place like this one, he ought to stick around and keep his pretty daughter out of trouble."

Hot tears shot into Vienna's eyes. "Father is in California; we're going to meet him there," she sobbed.

"Do you have a big brother or some grown man to protect you?" the women inquired.

Ashamed of her outburst, Vienna blinked away her tears. A fine picture she was presenting to these gallant pioneer women. "My brothers are small, but we do have a teamster," she said, steadying her voice. "My mother can hold her own in any situation. She happens to be a very brave lady, and I am trying to be like her."

"That's the spirit," the women praised her. "If you need us again, just holler and we'll be right over."

"Thank you most kindly." Vienna saw with surprise that the women returned to different companies. God had sent them, she felt. And He had sent that golden young man as a backup. Where had the rider come from? Where was he going? She hadn't remembered to thank him. How thoughtless of her! Without the women's help, he would have been the one to rescue her from the evil man's clutches.

Limbs trembling from the scary encounter, Vienna stirred the simmering bean soup, then resumed her knitting. Her brothers were still playing. Wrapped up in their noisy game, they hadn't noticed her predicament. Vienna was glad of it. The boys had gone through a rough time during their bout with the measles. They deserved a little happiness.

"Mama! Mama!" The boys stopped their play and ran toward the tall woman who marched between two dark-haired boys carrying well-filled sacks. Vienna heaved a sigh of relief. Mother was back!

The twins let the sacks slide off their backs. With perspiration trickling from pale foreheads, they proceeded to fill the bean and flour barrels in the wagon.

"Let me help you," Vienna offered.

"No, thank you," the twins refused proudly.

Vienna could tell that something was wrong. Mother's agreeable smile didn't fool her a bit. "Eat, Mother. You look exhausted." Vienna offered soup in a tin bowl.

Mother reached for the savory bean soup. "Thank you, daughter. We had success in town," she volunteered in her usual cheerful voice. "We purchased important food supplies and trinkets for our Indian hosts out west." Unrolling a kerchief, she revealed a heap of shining beads, whistles, and pins.

"How pretty!" Vienna gasped. "Look, Elisha!"

The twin dusted flour from his clothes. "The trader said we'll need these gifts because Indians are camping right across the river. People say the river is flooded and we'll find lots of graves out yonder. Some people aren't even going on."

Mother's glance stopped the boy's rattle. "You musn't frighten your sister with hearsay, Elisha."

Vienna had heard enough. The situation was worse than expected. No wonder Mother's forehead showed that deep worry line. Ever since that unhappy Sabbath day, Vienna had sensed a strange uneasiness in Mother.

"Did you post my letter?" Vienna asked.

"Yes, daughter. The trader will mail it."

"When do you suppose Priscilla will get my letter?"

"The trader could not say." Mother gave Vienna her penetrating gaze. "What happened while we were away?"

Vienna had been waiting for the question. About to spill her news, she reconsidered. The last thing Mother needed was an added worry. "The boys and I managed, Mother." She filled the boys' bowls, making certain Mother didn't see the warm flush that crept up to her hairline. More than ever, she appreciated the warm circle of her family. Together they could face anything, she hoped. She shuddered, thinking of the terrible aloneness she had felt when the bearlike man threatened her security.

She handed the hot soup to her brothers, who sat on the wooden ox yokes. Blowing over their steaming beans, they nudged one another playfully. The twins suddenly tossed their heads. Vienna followed the boys' focus of attention. Jeffrey was returning from town. The lad fairly swaggered, showing off a gun in its flashy holster. Vienna suppressed a chuckle. Jeffrey reminded her of a youngster carrying a brand-new toy. The thing kept slipping forward on his hip, getting in his way, and he kept pushing it back.

"Jeffrey got himself a gun, but he doesn't know how to carry one," Vienna snickered. She caught Mother's stern glance too late.

"Guns are no objects for fun, daughter. Guns can kill and maim. Let us not reinforce Jeffrey's new-ownership pride."

"Sorry, Mother." Vienna hadn't thought of guns in that way.

The gun gave Jeffrey a new air of self-importance. At yoking-up time next morning he swaggered like a general.

His "gee" and "haw" commands carried sharp authority. "A gun makes the man," he asserted. "Let the savages come! I'll shoot them dead."

Mother and Vienna exchanged distressed glances until the sight of the immense Missouri silenced their teamster. The wagon rumbled down a narrow path, crossed wet bottomland, and joined the long line of wagons waiting for the ferry. Vienna clutched her bonnet against the blowing, sand-carrying wind. She scanned the young men on horseback, searching for a tall rider on a golden chestnut mare.

"Nothing is moving," she stated flatly.

The wagon master galloped ahead. He returned with disheartening news. "The river is too high," he reported. "We shall wait until the water subsides."

"When can we cross?" Jeffrey shouted into the wind.

The wagon master shrugged. "Barring flash floods, the river may crest in a few days." He rode on, countering a barrage of agitated questions.

Frustration and confusion spread among the emigrants. Before day's end, many wagons turned back to Council Bluffs. Jeffrey attempted to turn the wagon, but Mother met him with determined resistance. "We shall go on, Jeffrey."

Jeffrey's face grew white, then red. "In that case, you better go on without me." He tossed the bullwhip handle to Elisha, grabbed his bundle and deserted. "See you back home in Michigan!" With that, he ran after a wagon that was heading back.

By nightfall the Brookses found themselves in the company of some 20 wagons, the sorry remnants of broken trains. For six nights the Missouri lulled Vienna into uneasy sleep. For six days she listened to tales of Indian massacres, starvation, and pestilence. The horror stories repeated one refrain: "The Plains are alive with Indians on the warpath."

At the edge of civilization, Vienna found she needed a stout heart to remember the journey's purpose. The family had nothing to go back to. Their hope lay in Father's promise to make a home for them in California. Mother looked toward the setting sun across the river that cut them off from everything familiar. Her face was unreadable.

"What are you thinking, Mother?" Vienna asked, fighting back her own conflicting feelings.

"Lot's wife." Mother looked troubled.

Husky ferrymen hailed the emigrants on the seventh day. Showing off bulging muscles under rolled-up sleeves, flashing white teeth in charcoal faces, they beckoned teamsters to drive aboard. Since nobody else volunteered to drive onto the flatboat, the Brookses went first. Mother's mouth became a straight line as the oxen stepped onto the swaying planks. The Black men assisted the family until oxen, wagon, and milk cows were loaded and secured. Mother kept the little boys close by her side. Vienna and the twins sat up front, watching the ferrymen push off.

The ferrymen steered toward the river's center, where strong currents whipped and whirled the flatboat about like some floating matchstick.

"No need to worry," the men grinned good-naturedly, reassuring Vienna. "The river is strong just now. Will be calmer soon."

Vienna gripped the wooden seat, holding on for dear life until the ferry moved out of the treacherous currents. Touching land on the opposite side, the family gave thanks for their safe landing. Well out of the river's reach, they waited for the other wagons. Since none arrived soon, they pitched camp within sight of the Indian encampment the trader had mentioned. The sun cast long rays onto the river, and still no ferry came in sight.

The grim reality hit Vienna during her evening chores: No wagons came across to join them! They were alone in the wilderness, alone with the Red men.

"I wonder what's keeping them, Mother." She warmed herself by the campfire. The wind felt nippy once the sun slipped below the horizon. She swallowed the cottony lump in her throat. Mother looked so forlorn!

"Nobody seems to be coming, daughter. It appears that everybody else turned back." Mother's words confirmed Vienna's fear. "We are without a teamster, leader, and wagon train, daughter. How can we manage?" Mother's voice broke. It was as though all spunk had left her.

"But Mother," Elisha protested, "I can handle the oxen."

"And I can lead them to pasture," Elijah offered.

"I can stand guard," Justus boasted.

"I can bring firewood," piped Orion.

"And I can dry the dishes," little Elmont chirped.

Mother embraced the boys. "You are *children*," she stressed. "Can five children do a man's job?"

"I am not a child," Vienna said. "*I* am a growing girl. Before long I shall be a young woman, and you can rely upon me."

Mother's eyes clouded over. She temporarily leaned on her children. "Do we dare travel on by ourselves? Can we truly guide the oxen? Dare we enter the land of the Red men in view of everything we have heard?"

"Yes!" the boys cheered.

"What about you, daughter? How do you feel?"

Vienna swallowed her fears under Mother's anxious gaze. Not since Father's departure had she seen Mother so distraught.

"How do you feel, daughter?" Mother urged.

Vienna groped for the right words. "We already have come so far, Mother. Wouldn't it be agony having to re-cross the rivers and all those horrible sloughs, when we are so far west already? God parted the Red Sea for the Israelites, and He helped us across many waters. Moses entered the wilderness by faith, and God stood by him."

Mother bent her head. "Let us pray for our safety."

The moaning wind brought strange sounds from the Indian encampment. Tepee poles loomed black against the darkening sky.

"O Lord, give us a sign." Mother's plea was a wrenching sob. She put the younger boys into the wagon bed, then tucked in the twins in their tent. She did not join Vienna in their bed under the wagon, but stayed outside. Securing the blankets around the wheels, she said, "Good night, daughter. Help me pray for a sign from God."

In the cold uncertainty of that night, Vienna watched her mother—her form revealed by fitful flashes of the campfire—kneeling beside a log, pleading earnestly for guidance. Mother's lips moved, and Vienna prayed with her.

"Lead, kindly Light, amid the encircling gloom,
Lead Thou me on;
The night is dark, and I am far from home;
Lead Thou me on."

Chapter Five
The New Teamster

Vienna awoke to rushing sounds. Believing she was back home in Michigan, she thought she heard wind in the pines. She pulled the cover over her chin. Had the coals died out in the fireplace? Mother always heaped ashes over the coals the night before, but sometimes the fire died anyway. She blinked. Not a spark! Soon Elisha would leave his trundle bed, bundle up, and fetch live coals from the nearest neighbor.

Why was the night so black? She groped at the wall of darkness surrounding her. The coarse weave of the blankets awakened her to reality. She shook herself. The swollen Missouri flowed past the wagon a short distance away. Was it only yesterday that the river had spewed them out into the wilderness?

Parting the blankets, Vienna saw her mother's kneeling figure. Acrid smoke hung about the campfire, and daylight dawned beyond the river. Had Mother stayed outside all night? Beads of perspiration showed on Mother's pale forehead. She was still talking with God.

Would Mother go on? Could they travel the strange and hostile road without a man's help? Tears stole into

Vienna's eyes. If only they could have journeyed west with Father! The masculine element had left the family when he departed. Vienna knew the boys missed sharing their little joys and pains with him. They asked Mother questions that only a man could answer, though Mother always did her best to satisfy the boys' every need.

Vienna sighed. Her parents' first child and the only girl, she'd been the apple of her father's eye. She got away with things for which her brothers were punished. She worked in the cornfield alongside the twins. She and the boys worked hard to hoe out their rows before sundown, knowing that Father would take away anyone's knife who failed to finish the row. The day Vienna failed she received a mild scolding. The day Elijah failed Father demanded the knife, and the 9-year-old hung his head in shame, knowing he was not big enough to do the work of an adult. Father disciplined the boys. Sparing the rod meant spoiling the child.

Vienna flinched. Hoofbeats and hideous yells jarred her. Blanketed riders swooped out of the nearby Indian village, making straight for the wagon. Mounted on fat ponies, they urged their horses at top speed, only to stop short by the dying campfire. The men's coppery faces were fancifully painted, and small, bell-like ornaments jingled about their ankles and necks.

Mother's head snapped back as the wild riders gathered around her. Blood curdled in Vienna's veins. She couldn't move. Mother rose and straightened her skirt. An uncertain smile trembling on her lips, she climbed up into the wagon and returned to fill the Indians' outstretched hands. The visitors noisily inspected Mother's beads, wheeled about, and left in peace.

"Get up, children! Let us do our chores and move on." Mother's face glowed in the morning light.

The shifting wind carried the scent of wildflowers like a sweet promise as Elisha goaded the oxen over a zigzag road to the crest of the bluffs. Looking back to the Iowa side, Vienna saw two lines of toylike wagons across the wide band of the Missouri, one headed for the crossing, the other turning back.

Mother laid her gentle hand on Vienna's shoulder. "You were right, daughter. Moses looked ahead to the Promised Land. He did not return to Egypt when the going got rough."

"The Israelites found their Promised Land, and so shall we, Mother." Vienna felt like singing, because she had been able to help.

They entered a prairie fanned by the morning breeze. Vienna ran ahead of the wagon. Finding wild tulips, bellflowers, and roses, she gathered the prettiest blossoms and offered them to Mother.

The prairie was treeless except for some brush and deciduous trees that grew along creeks and ravines. Once the morning breeze died, the sun beat down with scorching fervor. Vienna looked for water puddles to moisten her parched lips, but found none. She did find a few prairie peas, filled her pockets, and sucked on the juice.

Elisha steered the oxen to a small creek at noon. While he and Elijah loosened the animals to graze and chew their cud, the younger boys plunged into the water and quenched their thirst. Vienna filled a cup and gulped down the tepid water. She offered the refill to Mother.

A week and two major fordings later, Vienna spotted a wagon train to the rear during a noon stop. Her heart pounded. Was there anybody she knew? Perhaps Jeffrey, or John, the golden young man she'd met so briefly? The train's scout, a man with sharp features, caught up with the wagon. Steadying his black steed, rifle at the ready, he pulled back the canvas and peered inside.

"Where's your man?" he asked Vienna.

"We're traveling alone." Sitting on the wagon seat, Vienna countered the man's crude question with dignity. "We'd be thankful if you allowed us to join your party though."

He frowned at the splashing boys in the creek. "We're in a hurry to reach the gold mines, lass."

"Perhaps you could lend us a teamster," Vienna suggested.

"Haven't got much use for kids or women," he muttered.

"We can keep up if we have a teamster," Vienna boasted.

The scout turned his horse. "Have you got food for a man?"

"We got supplies at Council Bluffs. We counted on feeding our teamster, but he deserted."

The man looked around suspiciously. "You crossed without a man?"

"We did!"

His mouth fell open. "I'll be—"

When his company caught up, a teamster materialized. Vienna wished she'd kept her mouth shut. Her throat constricted the instant she saw—the bearlike man! He was no other than the brute who'd threatened her security at the Kanesville camp. He was bareheaded, sporting the most ornery red bristles she had ever seen. The sly glance he gave her sent icy shivers down the girl's spine.

"Red's the name," he said, looking her over.

"Where do you hail from?" Mother stepped beside them.

"Nowheres. Ain't got no home." He spit into his hands and yanked the reins from Elisha. "Shove over, son. Takes a man to do a man's job."

A quick appraisal of Red's buddies told Vienna that the family had fallen in with a motley crowd of male adventurers. Only one woman with her husband and 3-year-old son had crossed the Missouri and joined the men.

"A company of men, two women, and a girl." Mother voiced her distress out of Red's hearing range.

"We do need a strong teamster, Mother."

Mother looked at her strangely. "You appeared surprised at seeing Red. Have you met him before?"

"N-no," Vienna stuttered. She hoped Mother didn't see the flush that rose to her cheeks.

"We must suffer the situation for now," Mother decided.

Trouble started the moment Red picked on Elijah and his hens. Red hankered for fresh meat, and the family's two chickens fell victim to his lustful stomach. The chickens were barely digested when the teamster began talking about buffalo meat and pretty girls. Vienna walked beside Mother at the end of the wagon to avoid Red's burning looks.

On the Sabbath, Red and his company of roughs drank hard liquor and amused themselves with playing cards inside the wagon circle. Herders had taken the cattle to pasture, allowing the emigrants to do as they pleased.

"Gambling! May the Lord forgive these foolish men." Mother closed the Bible after the family's devotion.

Elijah sniffled. "I'll never forgive Red for killing my chickens."

Elisha sided with his twin, looking fierce. "And I'll hate our dear teamster forever and ever."

Mother drew the boys close. "We must forgive our wrongdoers just as our Lord forgave His tormentors."

Father's departure flashed through Vienna's mind. "But Mother, how can one forgive somebody who has hurt you so?"

Mother's eyelids flew open. "What are you saying, daughter? Who has hurt you?"

"If it hadn't been for Father, we wouldn't be in this mess. It's all his fault," Vienna accused.

The color drained from Mother's face. She released the twins. "Your father was ill, daughter. Have you forgotten the winter he lay in the cabin, shaking with fever?"

"He wasn't too ill to leave us," Vienna said bitterly.

Mother's hand flew to her mouth. "Daughter, what has been eating you?"

"It's true, Mother!" Vienna ran outside, tears blinding her. She ran to the shallow river along whose shores they had been traveling. The air was still under the cottonwood trees, the sky blue under a glorious June sun. Insects hummed in the dappled shade under the green canopy, and birds flew low over the glistening water.

Vienna slowed her pace. Why had she run? What was the matter with her anyway? The old feeling of being abandoned rushed back like a poorly digested meal, a bitter, acid lump in her stomach.

In her agitation she hadn't paid much attention to her surroundings. An animal broke through the brush, startling her. Branches crackled and snapped. Cattle grazed somewhere, judging by sharp tearing sounds in the grass. Spotting a calf through the branches, she rubbed her eyes in disbelief. There was no calf in their company! She stood still, trying to puzzle out the mystery. Where had the calf come from? It was a supersized calf, thick-headed and with an unusual build.

Deep-throated lowing sounds diverted Vienna's attention. A huge black cow was calling the calf. The cow was a powerful beast, hump-shouldered, and partially covered with long, shedding hair of a reddish color. The massive head sported short, upward-curling horns, quite unlike the Brookses' long-horned oxen.

Astonished, Vienna carelessly stepped on a branch. The cow uttered low grunts and began to paw the ground. Her wildly rolling eyes warned Vienna that she might charge. Vienna scrambled up the nearest tree.

"Help! Somebody help!" she yelled at the top of her lungs.

The cow was beneath her now, charging the tree trunk. Vienna clung to her branch for support. Vicious mosquitoes bit her hands and forearms, making painful red welts rise. Not daring to move, she endured the maddening misery. The huge black cow lingered below, her anger slow to subside. When she finally trotted off with her calf, Vienna spotted more hump-shouldered animals through

50

the green leaves. The great beasts snorted eagerly on their way to the water.

"Oh, no!" Vienna agonized. "Now I'll never get down." She couldn't judge how long she had clung to the cottonwood branch. Overheated, parched, her strength fading, she dreaded falling onto the back of some shaggy beast. The snorting animals broke through the brush and swam to a small island. Vienna held on with her last strength until the noises faded into the distance. Should she get out of it alive, she feared nobody would believe her adventure. Her brothers would tease her, suspecting she'd been charged by some imaginary phantom cow.

With peace restored—birds singing and insects humming—she felt hugely embarrassed. Served her right! Girls stayed home on the Sabbath day rather than running off like sulking babies. Her hands and forearms blurred into a mass of angry welts. Trying hard not to scratch, she headed for the river and cooled her smarting arms in the shallow water. As she splashed the silvery liquid onto her cheeks, she realized that the mosquitoes had spared her face. Smooth and unblemished, her countenance reflected back to her from the clear water. Framed by loose brown curls, dark eyes sparkling under russet brows, she looked like her mother, only the nose was babyish and the lips were full.

The prairie sun had tinted her skin rosy red, taking away the paleness of the Michigan winter. On Mother's insistence, she had spread homemade salve on her face and neck every morning. Made of herbs, the ointment shielded the skin from burning and double-functioned as insect repellent. Sudden tenderness for Mother overwhelmed Vienna. Mother always meant well. Without the hated salve, the insects would have bitten her face, and her eyes would have swollen shut so she couldn't have seen. And if that had happened, she'd have been doomed to sit beside their odious teamster and endure his foul presence.

A deep sigh heaved Vienna's chest. Supposing she'd

meet that golden young man again and he'd see her face disfigured. She couldn't bear the thought. Besides, she could have been gored or trampled. Many times Mother had impressed upon her children that "a mother animal is the fiercest creature alive. Don't ever come between a mother and her young."

"Stupid, stupid, stupid me," Vienna mumbled.

Chapter Six
Hero in Homespun

The next morning the entire company sighted the great hump-shouldered beasts of the prairie.

"Buffalo!"

The cry arose from hoarse throats. Men who owned horses sprang into the saddle. Kicking the flanks of their mounts, swinging rifles, they chased after meat.

"I'm gonna git me a great, big, bloody steak!" Red salivated into his snuff-smeared beard.

A thunderous roar drowned out Mrs. Miller's anguished cry, "They're coming this way!"

Vienna dashed out of camp. On a rise she saw them, a large herd of jostling quadrapeds whose pounding hooves shook the ground under her feet. The beasts galloped toward the rise, approaching with incredible speed.

"They'll trample us!" Red screeched.

"Let's head them off!" his buddies cried.

The men waved guns, sticks, and jackets in desperate attempts to head off the animals. Vienna, Mother, and the boys flailed aprons and shirts torn off their backs. A great bull knocked the most daring man to the ground. The man's cohorts lunged forward, yelling and waving blankets, succeeding in making the herd swerve. The army of woolly monsters thundered past the emigrants, smashing two tents, but missing the wagons.

After it was all over, Vienna retied the apron she had swung like a crazy person. Lightheaded and wobbly on her feet, she noticed a young man on the rise. Her hero from the Kanesville camp! Donning his jacket, he studied her with interest. Vienna held the gaze of those sky-blue eyes. Was she dreaming? Was it really John? Once again he'd appeared as if by magic and helped to keep her safe. Struck speechless, she couldn't convey her gratitude. A horse whinnied beyond the rise, and he disappeared over the crest, a tall, proud figure in the morning sunlight.

"Come, daughter! There is butter to be churned and breakfast to be made." Mother's call broke Vienna's trance.

"Who was that man on the rise?" Mother asked, searching the girl's face.

Cornbread

"Oh, Jeffery,—I thought Elisha was dying—I thought we'd all die from some terrible fever—and only because my brother ate dried apples!" Vienna threw back her head and laughed. And suddenly the entire family was laughing with her. Hot cornbread tasted wonderful, and the first part of the day's drive was fun.

1 Cup of stoneground cornmeal   ½ teaspoon salt
2 Cups boiling water (or hot milk)
1 tablespoon shortening

Preheat oven to 350 degrees. Scald by pouring water (or milk) into the cornmeal. Stir and beat to prevent lumps. Add salt and shortening. Spread on a cookie sheet in a round shape or cake ½ inch thick. Bake 35 to 40 minutes until crisp. (4 servings)

"I, uh, don't know, Mother. He must be with some other company." That hated flush once more spread to Vienna's hairline.

"Have you seen him before?" Mother probed.

"N-no." Vienna wished she had told Mother about the incident with Red at the Kanesville camp. Now she'd have to lie forever, she feared.

"You would tell me if something troubled you, daughter." Mother's statement sounded like a question.

"Y-yes, Mother," Vienna hedged.

While she churned butter, she recalled times when she wouldn't have dreamed of withholding news from Mother. Now she'd rather discuss her feelings with her Michigan schoolmate, Priscilla—or with somebody else her age—only there wasn't anybody she could talk with.

She watched Red and the other men light great fires in anticipation of a buffalo roast. Rifle shots cracked, making Vienna's head jerk. Triumphant yells rent the air as the hunters' overheated mounts dragged two fat buffalo cows into camp. Boasting about the hunt, the men eagerly stripped off the bullet-riddled hides to cut out choice pieces.

Vienna felt sorry for the big prairie animals who had blundered into the hunters' deadly path. Somewhere, the cows had left two orphaned calves. She told Red what she thought, but he was more impressed by the hunters' hair-raising details of the buffalo chase. While the hunters secured the steaks over the fires, Red and his friends extracted the liver, heart, and "marrow gut" from the cows' steaming bellies.

Vienna clutched Orion so he wouldn't see the final insult: the cutting out of the tongue. She was glad Mother kept little Elmont in the wagon. The twins and Justus, their tag-along younger brother, watched the gory scene, their faces expressing their horror. As if on command, the boys ran behind the wagon and retched. The Brookses did not participate in the men's lusty meal.

"Sorry, Red, we already ate." Mother declined Red's generous offer without further comment.

"Have it your way," Red muttered.

Mrs. Miller, the other woman in the company, her worried-looking husband, and their blond little son, Eddy, also spurned the smoking, blood-dripping meat offered at the end of a spit.

The next day the family had to do Red's work. The teamster was suffering a bad case of indigestion. He lay in his tent moaning, "Shouldn't 'a' eaten that fresh meat."

Elisha nudged Vienna. "Serves him right," he grinned.

"Don't let Mother hear you," Vienna cautioned. "She won't have you gloating over somebody else's trouble."

Elisha stuck out his tongue at her and hissed, "Schoolmarm!" He hated to be corrected.

Sometimes Vienna wished he were more like his twin. Elijah was easy-going and took corrections in stride. He was the twin who wanted a double measure of straw in his mattress, whereas Elisha slept on the hard ground without complaint.

Vienna nudged Elisha. "Look!"

Quiet Mr. Miller was approaching the rough character who was tending preparations for jerkying the buffalo meat. "How long will this delay last?" he asked. "My lead ox perished, and I may lose more oxen. We have passed the graves of people, and wolves howl at night, trying to get at us. If we sit around much longer we may all perish."

The rough sitting beside the smoky fire gave Mr. Miller a dirty look. "Won't take us no time to git to Californee. We're ahead of the suckers who're dilly-dallyin' at the river crossing."

"When shall we leave?" Mr. Miller challenged.

The rough shrugged. "Dunno. Why don't you go ahead by yourself?"

Mr. Miller blanched. "Alone in Indian country?"

"You said you was in a hurry." The man pulled a

medicine bottle from his coat pocket and took a swig.

Mr. Miller walked to his wagon, shoulders slumping. Even his son's cry of "Daddy, look what I found!" didn't cheer him. Eddy was constantly running off and finding things.

The company spent the next day smoking strips of flesh and hanging the jerky on ropes along wagon bows for the sun to finish the curing. Vienna, sickened by the sight of the disemboweled buffalo cows and the odors permeating the camp, needed to get away. Mother was visiting with Mrs. Miller, and the bigger boys had left to gather sun-dried buffalo chips that, as they'd recently discovered, fueled a wonderful fire.

Vienna waited for a break in the women's conversation, then asked, "Mother, may I take Orion to the river? I want to wash my hair."

Mother glanced up from her mending, looking uncertain. "What about buffalo, daughter?"

"The scouts said they haven't seen a single buffalo since the stampede," Vienna answered truthfully.

Mother hesitated. "Why don't you take Elmont, too. The boy needs a good scrubbing."

"Thanks, Mother!" Vienna lifted her delighted baby brother and gave him a big kiss. This was one of the rare occasions when Mother parted with the child.

Eddy broke away from his mother and clutched Vienna's skirt. "I wanna go too!"

Vienna laughed. "Is it all right, Mrs. Miller?"

"The boy is a handful," Mrs. Miller warned.

"I can handle him, don't worry." Vienna grasped Eddy's hand and carried Elmont on the other arm. She strolled to the river in a good mood. *This was going to be a fun day,* she decided.

Elmont received his scrubbing and Orion got his hair washed, but Eddy hid behind a tree when his turn arrived. "Come on out, Eddy," Vienna coaxed.

"Only if you promise not to wash me," Eddy pouted.

"All right, Eddy, I shan't touch you," Vienna sighed. Mrs. Miller was right, the boy was a challenge. As she washed her own hair she was relieved to see that the Miller boy joined her brothers.

Filtered sunlight caressed the wet strands of hair she spread around her shoulders. Tiny birds flew in and out of shrubbery on which she hung the wash she'd brought along. The place was filled with bird sounds, water sounds, and happy sounds of boys at play. Branches covered with fresh green leaves quivered in the gentle breeze, and through the sunlit foliage glimmered the sparkly, silvery water of the Platte River.

An enchanted place, a place to dream! Vienna sat on a rock, diary propped on her knee, watching insect hunters that gathered gossamer prey on swift wings. Parent birds flew in and out, fussing over their young in unseen nests above her head. Vienna's pencil rested idly in her lap. She closed her eyes, savoring the lovely surroundings, thanking God for this special day.

The peaceful spell was broken by the sound of breaking branches. Jumping up, she saw a young man leading a golden chestnut mare to the water. It was he, John! Her heart pounded. He hadn't seen her yet. Was her hair presentable? Were her clothes decent? She quickly pulled both sleeves over the ugly welts left by the mosquito bites.

Then Elmont's piercing scream sent her hurrying toward the boy. Nothing must happen to Elmont! Mother would never forgive her. "Why is he crying, Orion? Did he get hurt?" She rocked Elmont in her arms.

Six-year-old Orion pointed at Eddy. "He won't let him smell that flower."

Eddy crushed some plant in his fist. "It's mine!"

"Why, Eddy, God made flowers for everybody—for you, for me, even for the bees! God gave us pretty flowers because He loves us, and he wants us to love each other, too. We mustn't be selfish, Eddy, for God isn't selfish."

"But I saw it first," Eddy protested.

"Why don't you let Elmont smell it just once." Vienna set down her baby brother and tousled the Miller boy's hair. Eddy opened his fist, reluctantly holding up a crushed plant.

"That's a boy," Vienna praised.

In the rush to help Elmont, she had forgotten about John. Hearing noises behind her, she wheeled around. Her hero was striding toward her, bareheaded and without a jacket. His shirt collar was open, his sleeves rolled up. Vienna's heart jumped into her throat. Up close, he looked even better than from a distance. His neat, short-cropped hair dipped to his forehead. His square jaw gave him a manly, determined look. And, oh, his eyes!

His expression of amazement yielded to a smile that lit up the world. Eyes dancing under generous brows, even rows of white teeth flashing, he recognized her. He didn't say "Good day" or "It's you again." Instead he asked, "What seems to be the trouble? I heard a tot's cry and came to help."

Orion explained in Vienna's place. Vienna was eternally grateful, for she didn't trust her voice, owing to all the throbbing going on in her chest and throat. Picking up her diary and pencil, she sat down primly on a rock.

"Thank you for trying to help," she said cautiously.

His eyes sought hers in a way that reminded her of Mother. He nodded toward the pencil. "Can you write?"

"Of course!" It was the last question Vienna expected.

"Where did you go to school?"

"In St. Joseph County, Michigan, where we lived." Vienna's confidence returned. "I had a wonderful schoolmaster who guided me most ably in the wintertime. I know how to read, spell, and enunciate." Seeing John's interest, she continued, "The schoolmaster explained all the good lessons contained in *McGuffey's Eclectic Readers,* and Mother helped me with the difficult lessons at home. It was her dream to become a schoolteacher, you know."

"What changed her mind?" John asked.

"Father. She went west with him, pioneering first in Ohio, then in Michigan." Vienna hesitated. "Sometimes when I did really well at school, Mother called me a Scholfield," she confided.

John looked blank. "What does that mean?"

"It means that I am a good learner and business-smart. You see, my mother's folks own a woolen business in Connecticut, and she herself was educated in public schools there. Everybody knows that schools are good in New England." She realized that John was studying her. "Do you—want me to recite something?" she asked.

He laughed. "No, I believe you, but what about arithmetic? Can you count?"

"I should say so, sir!"

He laughed explosively. "The name is John. Please, don't call me sir."

"All right—John. And you may call me Vienna, although my full name is Vienna Brooks. And I wish to thank you ever so kindly for the, uh, assistance you gave me at the Kanesville camp."

He flashed a smile. "It was nothing, Vienna. The women there would have chased off that do-no-good anyway."

"And thank you for helping to drive off the buffalo," Vienna hurried on, afraid she'd forget something.

He shrugged. "Just happened to pass by. Anybody would have helped." He studied the boys playing at their feet. "Your brothers?" he asked.

"All but one."

"The rosy-cheeked little charmer, is he yours?"

Vienna noticed his fun-twinkling eyes. He was teasing her. She liked people with humor. "His name is Elmont, and he's my littlest brother. This one here is my brother Orion, and the third boy is Eddy Miller. His parents are traveling in our company."

"Which one cried?" John wanted to know.

"Little Elmont." Vienna scooped up her baby brother.

"May I give him a ride on my shoulders?" John asked.

"He would like that," Vienna answered, handing him over.

John hoisted the shy Elmont onto strong shoulders and gave him a fast ride. As Elmont uttered noises of supreme happiness Vienna couldn't remember when she had seen the tot so jubilant.

"I want to ride too!" Eddy demanded the instant John set Elmont down.

"How do you ask?" John prompted.

Eddy frowned. "Please?"

"That's better, but because our Lord said the last ones will be first, I shall take Elmont's brother next." Orion got a bouncing ride.

When John returned the merry youngster, Eddy threw a fit. "I don't wanna be last. I don't wanna get the last ride."

Chapter Seven
The BIG Z

❧───❧

You must forgive Eddy," Vienna pleaded. "He's an only child and not used to sharing." She saw that a shadow moved across John's face. "Did I say anything wrong?" she worried out loud.

The shadow quickly left John's face. "No, I merely remembered that I also was an only child until my little brother arrived. I was 4 years old and terribly jealous. Mother lavished all her affection on the baby, and I resented him."

"Oh, you poor man," Vienna commiserated.

He laughed. "Fortunately, I came to love my brother very much." He motioned to Eddy, who was cracking his little whip. "I hope Eddy also gets a little brother one day."

"I was thrilled when my brothers arrived," Vienna confessed. "I never needed cornhusk dolls, for the boys let me play mother with them." She sighed. "I only hope they don't resent me."

John's eyebrows shot up. "Why should they resent you?"

"Father spoiled me," Vienna blushed. "If the boys failed at something, they were punished. I wasn't."

"Is your father—dead?"

"He might as well have been for the last two years." Hot tears stung Vienna's eyes.

"You sound bitter."

"Do I?" Vienna sniffed. "He abandoned us, John; went off to California and left Mother alone with us children."

"You, Orion, and Elmont?"

"And Justus, who was 7, and the twins, Elisha and Elijah, who were 9. It was dreadful, John! We needed Father, and we missed him. Mother did a man's work on the farm and we helped, doing chores beyond our years."

"When you meet your father in California, all will be well, Vienna. Keep thinking, 'All is well!'" He lifted her chin.

She smiled up at him, all sadness gone. "I shall, John. I shall." She watched a bird fly into branches alive with the twitter of fledglings. "And you, John, where will you go in California?"

"Sutter's Fort in the valley of the Sacramento. Our wagon boss says the fort is the traditional stopping-off place for overland travelers. Captain Sutter, a Swiss gentleman, provided a haven for Americans when California was still under Mexican rule and closed to foreigners."

"Will you be a gold miner?"

"If I have to, Vienna. My goal is a business establishment. Before long, people will forget about quick fortunes and settle down. There's talk of land being available in California. Settlers need everything from plowshares to bolts of calico." Standing squarely planted, he gripped his shirt collar. "That's where I come in, Vienna. I'll furnish the needed supplies. And you, Vienna Brooks, where will you go?"

"Father is a lumberman near a place called Bidwell's Bar, on the *Rio de las Plumas*—Feather River in English. He'll make a home for us there."

"How fortunate to be greeted by a loved one! You may find that your father cares more for his family than you imagine."

"I suppose." Vienna didn't want to discuss her father anymore.

John grasped her fingertips ever so lightly. His warm, strong hands sent tiny shivers of delight through the girl. "Wherever you go, my dear Vienna, I'll find you. Remember that you have a friend in California who cares about you."

Wayside graves flashed through Vienna's mind. Small-voiced, she said, "What if we don't make it, John?"

Alarm jumped into his eyes. "You must not entertain such thoughts, Vienna. We both shall arrive in California, alive and well."

"I worry about you, John," she said. "Why must you travel alone?"

"My party is small; many wagons having turned back. Our scout deserted, so I help out scouting for water and pasture, and alerting our people to any possible dangers."

"How far behind are your people?"

"Two, three days. Our progress is slow, owing to wagon repairs and people recovering from disease. We shall attempt to catch up with your company."

How positive he is, she thought. "In case we should miss each other, how can you be found, John? I hear there are great mountains and ocean inlets the size of Lake Michigan in the sunset land where we're going."

Mischief hopped like marbles into his blue eyes. "Look for the BIG Z, capitalized. The BIG Z, that's me!" His expression changed, becoming serious. "The Z, last letter of the alphabet, is also the repository of the entire alphabet. It contains all of the world's treasures."

Vienna was intrigued. "Such as?"

He enumerated. "Action, Bible, Caring, Daring, Enquiry, Faith, Goodness, Home, Illumination, John!" Eyes twinkling, he continued, "Kindness, Love, Mother, Nature, Offspring, Prayer, Quietude, Stability, Taste, Uncles, Vienna!" The corners of his mouth moved earward in a huge smile. "Work, 'Xtraction (such as from books or plants), Youngsters." He caught his breath. "You see, Vienna, the Z contains them all."

"What happened to the R?" Vienna asked.

"Did I omit the R?" He looked sheepish. "Wait, I'll be right back!" He released her fingers, sprang to his feet, and hunted for his mount. The mare gave a joyful nicker, and Vienna listened to the plop of fading hoofbeats.

He was delightful. Ambitious, smart, goal-oriented. The BIG Z! She chuckled. How original of him to single out the last letter and elevate it to prominence. She hadn't particularly pondered the Z before, but the letter formed part of her mother's name, Eliza, and Mother certainly contained all the treasures of the world.

Vienna opened her diary, trying to concentrate on overdue entries. Approaching hoofbeats made her close the book. John's mare appeared between the cottonwood trees, chestnut coat gleaming in the river's shimmering reflection. John dismounted and slapped the mount's golden neck. He strode toward Vienna and handed her a wild rose.

"The R stands for Rosebud!" His white teeth flashed.

"For me?" Vienna inhaled the delicate perfume, knowing she had never smelled anything so sweet. Mixed emotions tugged at her, all going in different directions. Why had he taken the trouble to bring her this lovely flower? Why was this handsome young man, practically an adult, bothering with her—a kid? The question must have shown on her face.

"When I have my business—" He cleared his throat and started again. "When I have my business, I shall need a woman I can call my darling wife."

Vienna's head snapped.

"Me?"

"You are young, Vienna—15?"

"Barely 14." Vienna felt herself blush.

"I am 19. We both have time. You can grow up, and I can make a home for my dear old mother and younger brother. I can build up my business. When I post the BIG Z sign above the front door of my establishment, I will need a woman who excels in writing and arithmetic. Not any woman will do, mind you. What counts is love, faith, respect, cooperation. I shall need a God-fearing woman who raises children properly, and—one who'll get along with my mother."

Vienna beamed. "When I leave my family to get married, I hope to find a mother again. Why, a mother is the most precious person on earth!" She covered her mouth, embarrassed. "Next to a husband, I suppose."

He burst out laughing. "Oh, my dear Vienna, so much you have to learn."

"Are you making fun of me?" Vienna bristled.

He grasped her hand. "I should never do that! I respect you too much. You have been in my thoughts since I first saw you at the Kanesville camp. You have become precious to me in a very short time. Imagine, I've found a girl who does not flirt."

Her eyes flew open. "Whatever do you mean?"

"You cried for help when that man desired your attention, didn't you?"

"Any girl would have done that."

"Perhaps not. I found a girl who has courage, or else she wouldn't have confronted a stampeding buffalo herd."

"I—was afraid."

"So was I; everybody was. And I found a girl who is a peacemaker." He contemplated Eddy, who was wresting a pebble from Orion. "To get this boy to share something, anything, is an accomplishment."

"I did what came naturally."

"See what I mean? In each situation you did the fine and noble thing. Now that's a girl a man can take pride in!"

Vienna's head whirled. Could this be happening to her? In all her life she hadn't received such grand compliments.

"You're pretty besides," he added, eyes softening. "I

love the hair around your shoulders, so soft and shiny." He took a strand of her silky brown hair and let it slide between his thumb and forefinger. "You are like a rosebud, Vienna. Some day in far-off California you'll unfold your petals and reveal your full-grown beauty. I'll wait for that day if it takes half a dozen years."

"How will you find me?"

"By your scent. Like the honeybee, I'll find you. Like the homing pigeon, I'll seek you out." His voice became practical. "You're neat in dress and appearance, and your posture shows self-assurance. One can tell a lot by a girl's posture. Some girls slouch, showing a lazy, noncaring disposition. Not you! You carry yourself well."

It was true, Vienna realized. She was conscious of her posture, taking great pains to sit and walk erect. She regretted not having Mother's long-waisted figure. She rather suspected she'd grow up to be stocky and square-shouldered like her father, perhaps tending to put on weight later in life. Good posture made her look tall. Slouching proved all too easy, but Mother's admonitions helped. And now all her efforts to keep her shoulders straight had paid off: John had noticed!

"Whatever I have, John, I consider a God-given gift."

"And God gave you a voice like a bell," he added.

Vienna felt like singing. All her life she'd been imitating Mother's beautiful voice. She'd always enjoyed listening to Mother, and now John enjoyed listening to her!

That night she listened to the call of a whippoorwill and the soft hooting of an owl. At the campfire outside, a fistfight was in progress. Fights among Vienna's traveling companions erupted over the slightest provocations. She ignored the men's offensive language.

Parting the blanket curtain, she glimpsed the night sky through the wheel spokes. The sky was starry, serene, eternal. It cared nothing about the rough men's quarrel. Was John seeing the same stars this very moment? Was he thinking of her? His rosebud rested securely between the pages of her diary. She had left the paper blank. No words sufficed to describe the exquisite feeling his presence sent skipping to the ends of her fingers and toes. The rosebud's sweet perfume would forever remind her of that special afternoon at the Platte River.

The morning sun rose hot and sultry. The skies were clear, but a storm was brewing. The men abandoned the last strips of smoking jerky in search of pasture for the bellowing animals. Filled water caskets jolted in the wagon box, and a large kettle of Mother's herbal tea rattled behind the driver's seat.

Knowing that each step was taking her farther from John filled Vienna with unspeakable sadness. She trudged over wild country, sidestepping prickly-pear cactus, bleached buffalo bones, and discarded belongings left by earlier wagon trains. The sun burned and perspiration collected between her shoulder blades. When Mother put the cranky little boys to bed, Vienna herself yearned for a resting place. If only she could sleep maybe she wouldn't worry so much about John.

A cloud rose in the west, growing to giant proportions. It devoured the sun and shook gusts of wind from its towering heights. Teamsters rushed the wagons into corral formation and hurried with the evening chores.

"That's it for today!" Red yelled, hastening to his tent, the wind tearing at his hair and beard.

With wagons secured and animals safely inside the circle, everybody needed sleep. It was then that Mrs. Miller screamed in the lull between thunder claps. "Help! Our little Eddy is missing!"

"Fool woman coulda watched out for that boy!" Red cursed.

The men grudgingly yielded to Mrs. Miller's pleas and formed a search party, but blinding lightning strikes and drenching rain forced them back empty-handed.

Vienna huddled inside the wagon with her mother and brothers. Stillness, punctuated by long-drawn howls, followed the storm's fury.

"Do you hear what I hear, Mother?" Vienna asked.

"Yes, I hear the great wolves of the prairie." Mother sounded amazingly calm. "Let us pray for Eddy's safety. If we love God, we are under His protection always. He will close the mouths of wolves if necessary. He will provide shelter for Eddy until the child is found."

"But, Mother—"

"Hush, let us not be unduly anxious." Mother laid a comforting arm around Vienna.

Vienna prayed for John, as well as for Eddy. Near daybreak they heard Mrs. Miller's distraught cry, "Please, look for our son again, please!"

When the men refused, Vienna approached Red, who emerged wet and grumbling from his tent. "You cannot be so heartless as to refuse Mrs. Miller. Please look for Eddy again!"

"You're crazy, lass," Red brushed her off. "That kid has had it. Wolves got him for sure."

Mother drew Vienna away. "We shall search for Eddy ourselves. Come, children!" She hoisted the sleepy-eyed Elmont on her arms and Vienna led Orion. The Miller and Brooks families fanned out and combed the camp's surroundings.

Eddy was nowhere to be found. Vienna gave up. Red was right, the wolves had gotten the child. She shuddered at the thought of sharp fangs and snapping jaws. Then a voice rang out. She looked up. A horseback rider popped up in the sagebrush.

"Are you people looking for a child?"

"He's got our Eddy!" Tall, lean Mr. Miller, his haggard face showing the strain of the awful night, broke into a run.

Vienna squinted against the rising sun. The rider's hat was drawn over his face. A child's limp body dangled across the wet horse in front of him. Vienna's breath caught. "Oh, Lord, take pity on the parents. Don't let Eddy be dead!"

Elisha beat Mr. Miller to the horseback rider and received the child in his receptive arms.

"I found the tot under a clump of sage," the horseman explained. "He's chilled. You'd best tend to him at once."

Mother and Mr. Miller rushed Eddy to the wagons without a second's delay. The rider tipped his hat and turned his rain-soaked horse. Nobody paid further attention to him in the general excitement.

Nobody, except Vienna.

Chapter Eight
New Departures

Wet sagebrush sent pungent odors afloat on the morning breeze. Stillness lay over the prairie as if all of nature waited for the rescuer to reveal his face. The *clip clop* of hoofbeats sounded like the gentle rocking of a baby's cradle as the rider directed his horse toward the girl. Stopping, he lifted his hat.

She gave a little cry. "John!"

"Vienna!" He dismounted, flashing his dazzling smile. "I ought not to have come your way," he explained, "but my matches got wet. Searching for dry weeds to light a fire, I found Eddy moaning under a clump of sage. He was gripping a whip in his tight little fist." He pointed to an object protruding from his saddlebag.

"He loves that little whip!" Vienna exclaimed. "Oh, John, I am so grateful to see you! I feared you were lost in the storm."

He looked at her appreciatively. "I had to return."

"Why, John?"

He faced her, blue eyes intent. "Without meaning to rush you, Vienna, what are your feelings in regard to me? I must know. You need not promise anything, and you're not bound to whatever you say. But I must know what you think of me and my future plans."

Vienna's heart thumped. Her feelings for this golden young man? How could she express feelings she hadn't had time to sort out? She saw herself as a tiny girl, giggling and squealing while being whirled around Father's head, feeling blissfully secure in his strong and loving arms. "Your presence makes me feel happy," she admitted. "What else do you want me to say?"

"About the BIG Z!" His adam's apple moved up and down. "Would you have any objections to becoming the— the wife— and partner of a businessman?"

Knowing she was blushing, Vienna studied a puddle in the white sand. "No objections, John. And I certainly would cherish my husband's mother."

"What about children?"

"If the Lord grants me children, I shall be happy to bring them up in His commands."

"Yippee!" He tossed his hat high into the air and caught it with a flourish. "Let's go tell your mother."

"What? Now? She, uh, doesn't even know about you." Seeing his long face, she added, "Yet."

"No better time than the present," John decided. "Come, let us get her blessing."

"Wh-what are you going to tell her?" Vienna fretted. For some strange reason, she couldn't predict her mother's response. Such news had never been sprung on Mother before.

He laughed. "That I hope to win you as my darling wife." With his mare trotting beside him, he led her toward the camp. But no camp was left over the rise. Only the Millers' and Brookses' wagons remained. John put a comforting arm around Vienna's shivering body. Voices drifted up from behind the Millers' wagon, where Eddy's father was comforting his hysterical wife.

They found Mother in the Millers' wagon. Standing beside John at the foremost hoop, Vienna hoped to get immediate attention. Mother barely looked up. She was busy urging herbal tea down Eddy's throat. "Red and his companions departed without us, daughter, and the Millers will turn back as soon as Eddy comes around." Mother appeared upset.

"Mother, this is John! He's—"

"Eddy's rescuer." Mother's gaze measured the young man in the homespun. "Thank you ever so kindly, John. May the Lord bless you for saving the Millers' only child."

Vienna broke in. "Mother, John has come to—"

John took over. "Mrs. Brooks, ma'am, Vienna and I—"

Eddy's eyes fluttered at the worst possible moment. "Where's my whip?" Eddy whined. "I want my whip. I lost it and looked for it. Then dogs came in the night, and I whipped them away."

Mother's hand flew to her mouth. "What dogs, Eddy? There aren't any dogs around here."

"There are too! Big ones. They look real mean."

John jumped from the wagon and fetched the small whip. Eddy, color returning to his face, gripped the toy. He was still clutching the whip when Mother stepped from the wagon.

"The child is all right," Mother told the Millers. Turning to Vienna, she suggested, "Why not help your brothers round up the oxen, daughter. Time is of the essence. We must travel hard and fast to catch up with our company."

"But Mother, John—"

"Sorry, daughter, I must assist the Millers. Let us talk some other time."

"Can't we travel with the Millers, Mother? John can lead us to his company." Vienna's hopes rose sky high.

Mother swept past her, speaking in her sharpest tones. "We must make speed, Vienna. Your father is expecting us in California."

Vienna looked at John in frustration. His pained expression yielded to a smile. "There'll be a better time and another place to arrest your mother's attention, Vienna. Remember, *all is well.*"

Hours later, Vienna sat on the wagon seat. Elisha's "Gee" and "Haw" annoyed her. The oxen plodded in the tracks of Red's company, balking occasionally under zigzagging lightning and explosive thunderclaps. Rain pelted the prairie all around them without touching the wagon. She glimpsed the perfect arch of a rainbow without joy. Would she ever see the golden young man again? His tender farewell lay miles behind her. All she had left was John's rosebud. She fingered the diary on her lap, wishing fervently she could discuss John with Mother. If only she had told Mother about the incident at the Kanesville camp. If only she had leveled with Mother after the buffalo stampede. Now how was she going to explain John?

She broached the subject. "Mother, John really wanted to speak with you."

"Eddy's rescuer. Oh, yes, a fine young man. The Millers' will thank him forever for saving their son."

"Mother, John wanted to speak with *you.*" Vienna's frustration mounted. Mother wasn't making it easy for her.

Mother looked at her sharply. "Did he say what about?"

"Y-yes," Vienna ventured. "He plans to establish a business in California."

"A business!" Mother's eyebrows arched.

Vienna plucked up her courage. "He says he's looking for a girl who can help him— one he can make his— his wife."

"He will no doubt meet some able young woman on his journey."

Vienna loathed the way Mother said *woman.* She tried again. "John isn't looking for just any girl, Mother. He needs one who is good at figures and writing."

"How soon does he expect to establish his business?"

"He's very smart, Mother. It won't take him any time at all to—" She stopped herself, seeing the steep line on Mother's forehead.

"Did he ask *you* to marry him?"

"Y-yes, Mother."

"You are too young, daughter."

"He'll wait until I'm older, Mother. Besides, you married young, and Father was older than you."

"That was different."

"But, Mother!"

"Men give young girls many sweet promises, Vienna." Mother spoke in even tones. "A clever young man can sometimes persuade trusting parents to let their young daughter depart with him. Out West, there is no telling what can happen to a girl. Without family to help her, where can she go when her husband is cruel?"

"Oh, Mother, John would never be cruel!"

"Where can she go when she expects a baby and there is nobody around to help? Having babies is a dangerous undertaking. Many women die in childbed."

"But Mother, you had lots of babies!"

"I was lucky—and strong."

"I'm strong, Mother."

"Enough of this idle chatter, daughter. The journey has been rough on you, I know. But you are still only a child. Forget this young man and keep your mind on the journey."

"You're not being fair, Mother! If only you had talked with John you'd know that he's trustworthy."

She jumped from the wagon, sobbing. She hated the salivating oxen, the creaking wagon wheels, the smelly jerky Red had hung along the wagon bows.

At dusk, she reluctantly took her seat on the wagon. Elisha traveled on in the growing dusk; Mother's orders! At midnight they glimpsed white-topped wagons under a sky swept clear of clouds.

"Who's there?" the guard yelled.

"It's us, the Brookses," Elisha yelled back.

"You gotta stay outside."

"Can't we put our oxen in the circle?" Elisha pleaded.

"We don't want them to run off with any buffalo or Indians."

Always protective of his pets, Elisha braved the guard's temper. The guard stomped to a tent. "Hey, Red! Your petticoat party is back."

Red pushed open the tent flap. Fumbling with his suspenders he muttered, "Useless women and kids. Figured they stole my jerky."

Elisha snapped a reply, but Mother hushed the boy. "We should be grateful if you would kindly put our cattle inside."

"Grateful! That so?" Red put his muscles to a wagon tongue while Vienna helped the twins with unyoking. His language shocked Vienna as he goaded the oxen into the wagon circle.

"Why must we endure his company when we could be traveling with—" She didn't dare add "John."

Mother sounded weary. "Red's company is protection, Vienna. After all, the men risked their lives to save us from the stampeding buffalo."

"They saved themselves, Mother."

"Nevertheless," Mother cut her off.

Red took the reins the next morning. His sly glances at the "useless women" showed that he was happier to have them back than his rudeness indicated. Not finding grass for the animals, the company swerved again toward the Platte. Once in sight of the river, tempers flared. Swelled by flash floods, the Platte was deep and treacherous.

"Hey, what's doing?" Red hailed the teamster ahead.

"The ferry's washed away," the teamster shouted.

Several men swam to an island in the stream's center and attempted to haul the first wagon over with the aid of long ropes. Vienna's cry died in her throat as the wagon overturned, carrying one of the men to a watery grave. Another man was swept away by the swift current. A daredevil rider swam out, and the drowning man succeeded in grasping the horse's tail. Rider, horse, and hanger-on survived, much to Vienna's relief. How was John going to fare when his small party crossed over?

For two days the men tried various methods of getting the wagons across. The Platte's rapid current and quicksands defied their united efforts. A cheer rose from hoarse throats when two ferrymen arrived with timber. Everybody, including the twins and Justus, went to work. Armed with woodworking tools, they labored for a week, building a raft large enough to hold a wagon.

Vienna waited for John to catch up. *Will he come this way?* she wondered. *Will he know how to find me?* "O dear Lord, please let me see him one more time," she sighed.

She played post office and advertised her whereabouts. Buffalo skulls and large, sun-bleached bones afforded wonderful opportunities to inscribe her name. Placed conspicuously by the trailside, they couldn't be missed. New hope filled her, chasing away the blues. John's party might draw up from behind and, hope of hopes, they'd travel together to the land of the Golden West.

Returning wagon trains exchanged warnings and information. They cautioned of dangers ahead. Vienna told them, "If you see a company coming this way, please tell them that you met Vienna Brooks—that's me. We're friends of the Millers and—" She usually stopped at this point, aware of Mother's frown and Red's suspicious look.

"You got a young man somewheres?" Red asked.

"You'd best mind your driving," Vienna told him.

"You stuck on Jeff, the milk face?" Red persisted.

"Never you mind!" She wished the teamster would give her peace.

He swung the bull whip over his head, then lashed it down over the oxen's heads. "Mebbe you been seein' that Kanesville feller?"

Vienna's face grew hot. She didn't wish to discuss John with the grimy teamster. To escape Red's pestering, she poked around abandoned items—harnesses, trunks, camping utensils, mining machinery, and grave markers.

Chapter Nine
Indians!

A roaming band of Sioux warriors swooped past on wind-swift horses, then hung on the company's flanks. Nightly, the men parked the wagons in a circle, stretching chains across the openings to safekeep the stock. Armed sentinels with horses, hobbled or picketed, kept up vigils a short distance from camp.

Bedding down her tired body on the hard ground, Vienna listened with rising alarm to her brothers' prayer: "If I should die before I wake, I pray the Lord my soul to take." *With Indians on their tracks, what are our chances of survival?* Vienna asked herself. Fear of a violent death lodged in her innards. Returning companies had spoken of scalpings and massacres. Were Indians moving stealthily outside this very minute, noiseless and unseen like spirit creatures?

"Mother?" Vienna spoke in a little girl's voice.

"Yes, daughter?" Mother's hand sought Vienna's. "We must keep faith, daughter. Keep your heart serene and not a hair will be bent on your head."

"But what if the Indians get us?"

"Let us seek God's grace, daughter. His grace brings inner peace."

"How does one get that peace, Mother?"

"The rules are simple. Love God above everything, and your neighbor as yourself; keep His commandments."

An ox snorted in the circle and a chain rattled. The guard's command sounded rough. "Who goes there?"

Nothing stirred. Only the coughing and shuffling of the corraled cattle answered. Vienna's fear yielded to an irrational hope. Was John out there? Had he found her at last? She pushed the blankets aside.

Mother pulled her back. "Stay inside, daughter."

"Just looking, Mother!"

No horseback rider appeared beyond Red's tent. Only the guard's hobbled horse made a dim outline, and his boots thumped as he inspected his side of the corral. Vienna spent a sleepless night.

Breakfast chores put beads of perspiration on her forehead. Cumulus clouds dotted the sweeping sky dome. The blue patches reminded her of John's eyes. Backward glances revealed clouds radiating golden sunrays. The panorama stretched endlessly without a tree in sight. Vienna yearned for the sight of trees. Sometimes she thought she was going mad. How soon could they expect to glimpse the stately pines Father had written about? Nothing indicated that California was getting closer.

Climbing a ridge at midday, Vienna saw the blue sky windows disappear behind dirty cotton-wad clouds. Fat raindrops hit the ground, and suddenly her clothes were wet. The shower passed, leaving odors of damp earth. Hot sunshine dried her clothes as she hastened back to the wagon.

"Whoa!" teamsters commanded. Brakes screeched and horses gave shrill neighs. Gray brush and red outcroppings came alive as Indians materialized on both sides of the wagons, shocking Vienna with their untamed presence. Where had they come from? Why hadn't she seen them before?

A halt was called for a council of war. The roughs decided to drive on with guns ready for action. Mother hustled the boys into the wagon, and Vienna followed her brothers headlong. Red hurtled himself into the wagon box behind the girl, telling Elisha to handle the team. While the 11-year-old got the oxen going, Red crowded Vienna. Bedlam broke loose outside. Indians uttered blood-curdling whoops. A whip cracked, and Elisha screamed like a boy gone mad.

"Leave my oxen alone! How dare you hit my Brock?"

The oxen jumped and struggled, threatening to overturn the wagon. Shots exploded, Indians yelled, teamsters uttered unrepeatable words. A wild clatter of horses' hooves followed, then sudden quiet.

Red lifted his head. "What happened?" He appeared in no hurry to move away from Vienna. She punched his barrel chest with feelings of disgust. "Get out of here!"

Mother, who had remained at Elisha's side, braving arrows and tomahawks, looked in the wagon box and took the situation in at a glance. She lit into Red with unexpected vehemence. "Let go of my daughter, you unholy man! Don't you ever come near the girl again!"

Grumbling, Red crawled onto the driver's seat, where he took a tongue-lashing from the shaken Elisha. Vienna felt faint. The stench of Red's unwashed presence hung in the wagon, and his bloodshot eyes followed her yet. She didn't know which she dreaded more, Indians or Red.

The native horsemen had galloped away on wind-swift mounts. Mother's observation that none of the Indians had used a deadly weapon convinced Vienna that these Indians couldn't possibly have been "hostile savages."

An Indian village loomed ahead at camping time. A new council called by the men decided that the party should stop for the night because the oxen were too exhausted to travel on. Vienna thought it strange that once again they camped within sight of an Indian village. Standing high on the wagon seat, she saw lodgepoles extending above buffalo skin tents. Smoke curled up from clever openings on top and from outdoor fires. Strangely adorned men, women, and children milled about, making the village appear as busy as a lumbering town on some festive day.

Going about her evening chores, Vienna heard the laughing and chattering sounds of women. Memories of church socials surfaced in her mind, for she hadn't heard women's light-hearted chatter in ages.

Mother's face lit up at the sight of approaching squaws. "Let us welcome our guests, daughter."

The squaws stopped short, looking uncertain. Mother sat down on an ox yoke and motioned for the women to join her on the ground. The women had brought bone needles, sinew thread, and prepared buffalo skins. Losing no time, they beckoned Vienna and her brothers to take off their footwear.

Vienna's feet smarted as she pulled off her tight shoes. Sore spots reddened her toes and the sides of her feet. She rubbed the painful spots. The squaws measured six pairs of feet, then commenced to fashion moccasins.

Vienna watched the old squaw who was sewing her moccasins. She liked the woman, even though her face and hands were dark and leathery and her long hair was straggly. The squaw pulled the sinew thread through her few teeth before threading it nimbly into the bone needle. Crinkles radiated around her prominent cheekbones and her dark eyes twinkled in fun.

Slipping into the moccasins, Vienna sighed with pleasure. The slippers were wonderfully comfortable. Fashioned of a single piece of leather, they conformed perfectly to the contours of her feet. The foot portion, made of supple yet rugged leather, wrapped up over her toes, and the rawhide lacing permitted future adjustments.

"Look, Mother, they really fit!" she chortled. "How can I pay for my shoes?"

"Leave that to me, daughter."

Mother's trinkets had been dwindling. Vienna was curious what she'd trade off this time. Mother produced fancy pins from her sewing kit and showed them to the delighted squaws. Receiving seven fancy pins in exchange for each pair of moccasins, the squaws left, laughing and chattering. Before long, they returned and demonstrated that one squaw had received eight pins. Now they all wanted eight! Mother granted their request, an amused smile lingering on her pretty face.

Vienna was still laughing when hoofbeats approached the camp. In the glow of the campfire, the bareback riders indicated they wanted to buy Vienna's brothers. Sign language established the price—a pony for each boy. Mother indicated she did not wish to sell. Seeing their long faces, she passed out consolation gifts—an old hoopskirt, Father's starched white collars, Vienna's umbrella, and tin whistles.

The proud princes of the Plains tried on skirt and collars, opened and closed the umbrella, then whistled and danced with glee. Vienna broke into laughter. It was too funny. A tall youth with rippling muscles and a pleasing countenance stood aside, eyes riveted on Vienna. When he finally led two handsome ponies to Mother, his overtures made clear the splendid ponies were offered in exchange for the girl. Vienna gripped Mother's arm. The youth's dark eyes betrayed intelligence, and his demeanor showed respect. Vienna hid her panic. She didn't want the young Indian to think he was repulsive to her.

"Get me out of this, Mother," she whispered. "I don't want to become an Indian squaw."

Mother spoke and gestured her answer. "I am sorry, but the girl is not for sale." She offered a blanket and a pint of precious sugar for one of the ponies and its hackamore bridle. The youth dipped a cautious finger into the sugar bowl and carried a pinch to his lips. Tasting the sweetness, he made surprised noises. He slung the blanket over his naked shoulders and strutted about with great satisfaction. The bargain was sealed and he left, but not before sending regretful glances at Vienna.

Elisha couldn't wait. "Who's the pony for, Mother? Are *you* going to ride it? Is it for *Vienna?*"

Mother laughed. "It's yours, Elisha, and your brother's—if he cares to ride the spunky little horse."

"Not me!" Elijah assured her.

Elisha hoisted himself onto the pony's back for the first horseback ride of his young life. To Vienna's amazement the pony shot away, bucking and bolting straight to the Indian village, with Elisha hanging on for dear life.

"Come back, Elisha!" Mother shouted.

"It was a trick, Mother! They got their pony back, plus our boy, for free," Vienna exclaimed.

Dogs barked furiously at the village. Mother rushed to Red's companions and urged them to rescue the boy. The men shook their heads.

Red was more emphatic. "Serves that sassy kid right. Let the Indians make a meal of him!"

"I shall go by myself!" Mother declared.

Soda Biscuits

The wagons rumbled past the lumbering village to the sounds of cheers, prayers, and hymns of settlers who came to see them off. Women wept on seeing the children on the wagons. One kind-hearted lady handed up cold biscuits. Mother accepted the gifts, visibly moved. "Bless you sister!"

2 cups of flour, sifted   ¾ cup buttermilk
½ teaspoon baking soda
½ teaspoon salt   4 tablespoons shortening

Preheat oven to 375 degrees. Sift together all dry ingredients. Cut in shortening with knives or cutter. Add buttermilk to make a soft dough. Knead one minute. Pick off biscuit-sized pieces and flatten and mold with hands. Bake 12-15 min.

(8 biscuits.)

"Don't leave us, Mother!" Vienna wailed. "The Indians will take us while you're away, and they'll keep you, too."

Mother reconsidered. She stoked the fire and let it burn brightly in its ring of stones. Perching on an ox yoke, she watched the village. Dogs no longer barked. Odors of roasting meat drifted from the Indian encampment. Chanting and rattling noises made ominous sounds in the night.

What are they doing to Elisha? Vienna fretted. *Was Red right? Did Indians cook White boys? Were they celebrating his capture and feasting on his flesh?* Goose bumps rose on her arms. The moon rose behind whitish clouds, hiding what might be a ghost dance for her brother.

Vienna jumped up. She couldn't stand it anymore. "Let's march into the village and find out what happened."

"Listen, daughter!" Mother's drawn features flickered in the firelight as agonizing screams pierced the night. Ponies were coming their way.

"They're coming to get us, Mother!"

Mother rose to her full height. "Hide in the wagon, daughter; keep out of sight."

Vienna didn't have to be told twice. She scrambled into the wagon to join her terrified brothers.

"Help! Help!" The voice was Elisha's. And suddenly a band of Indians pranced about the fire. Vienna peeked out. She couldn't believe what she was seeing. Indian youths had brought back her brother. Laughing merrily, they helped him off his pony, tied the snorting little horse to the wagon, and galloped off.

Red stuck his scraggly head out of his tent. "Shoulda kept that worthless boy," he grumbled.

"You just mind your own business!" Vienna retorted.

Elisha kept strangely quiet about his misadventure. He headed for his tent, looking like a ghost. Only the pony's presence and the soft moccasins on her feet reminded Vienna of the misunderstood Indians.

Chapter Ten
Saucy Girls

Gunshots wakened Vienna on the Fourth of July. Hunters were dragging three bloodstained antelope into camp amid loud cheers. Traveling north of the Platte, with bustling Fort Laramie (Wyoming) behind them, the men decided to celebrate Independence Day with fresh meat, "come hell or high water." A leader read the Declaration of Independence, then directed the preparation of the game.

Red and his buddies amused themselves with a noisy game of cards, while passing the brandy bottle around. Vienna had been avoiding Red. The tension between the teamster and her had become unbearable. Mother also kept her distance from the vile man, and Elisha spurned the wagon seat behind his beloved oxen. Red even had turned off the leaders who, in angry arguments, called him a coward and troublemaker.

The boys received Mother's permission to leave camp. While the twins led "Nippy" to pasture, Justus and Orion rode on the hobbled pony's back. Vienna hoped for a quiet moment to update her diary. She felt restless. Something was amiss, but she didn't know what. Earlier entries seemed childish to her now. "I'm not the same girl who left

Michigan," she muttered. Red's buddies rudely jarred her out of her reverie.

"Betcha that lass would slap your face," they teased each other.

"Happens to be crazy 'bout me, that 'un," Red bragged.

"Crazy! That so?" one of his buddies roared.

"You call me a liar?" Red flared.

"A liar and a yellowbelly."

Vienna fidgeted. *Where was Mother?* Little Elmont had run off to watch the roasting antelope, and Mother had run after him. Then Vienna spied Mother through the wagon wheels, restraining the squirming Elmont while talking to the leader who had read the Declaration of Independence.

Red staggered to his feet. "You think I don't dare? Just watch me!" Belching, he stumbled to Vienna's seat.

"Mother!" Vienna cried, and fled into the wagon.

Red countered his buddies' uproarious laughter with abusive comments. A gunlock clicked, and Vienna hurled herself onto the wagon floor. Gunfire exploded outside, Mother screamed, and the leader yelled a command. Mother's voice cut through the clamor.

"We are leaving this company! We shall take our chance with wild beasts and Indians rather than remain in the presence of this degenerate man."

"What about my payoff, after all I've done for that woman?" Red clambered onto the wagon. Flashing a suspicious eye, he greedily snatched two blankets and various food supplies that he tossed into the bean barrel. "It's all your fault, you wicked wench," he barked at Vienna as he dragged the barrel from the wagon.

Eliza Ann Brooks and her family left the wagon train at gunpoint.

Insects hummed by the little stream where the family pitched camp. Alone in a vast solitude somewhere near the Rocky Mountains, Vienna fought her smothering panic. During the night she listened to the howling of wolves, the only sounds in that vast stillness. At sunrise she watched with feelings of despair as the roughs' white-topped wagons passed them. She loved company. Any company was preferable to being alone in this wilderness infested with alkali, prickly pears, and rattlesnakes.

Without the beans Red had claimed for himself, the family went on short rations. The oxen fared no better. Wagon trains hurried past in a mad rush to reach the Sierra Nevada before the first snowfall closed sky-high mountain passes. Their oxen, cows, mules, and horses clipped pastures bare. The Brookses' oxen tottered behind the trains, sluggishly obeying the twins' piping treble. One by one, the wagons passed and faded into the setting sun.

Fourteen miles a day is a good day's journey, Vienna noted. *Too slow to keep up!* The road was littered with smelly cadavers. Skeletons covered with shrunken hides sometimes sheltered the boys from howling storms. One day Vienna counted 105 headstones. Signs on the fresh mounds read, *Died of Cholera, 1852.*

On the Sweetwater River a band of Indians chanced upon the lone family resting on the Sabbath day. Alarm signals flew. Through sign language, they learned that the tribe was moving camp in search of better hunting grounds and did not wish to harm the White mother. Vienna watched cautiously as the Indians erected their tepees. The two unlikely parties traveled together for a week.

When their ways parted, Vienna wrote, *Red men in rich robes of bear and panther skins, decked out with fringe and feathers. Red men without robes or feathers. Handsome squaws in elegant mantles of bird skins, tattooed and adorned with beads. Ugly squaws in scanty rags without beads. Papooses rolled in ornamented cradles, grinning from the backs of their mothers. Toddling papooses without a rag and unwashed. Ponies hidden under huge burdens; packs of dogs creeping under wonderful loads.*

And in the rear, she mused, *gaunt oxen, a creaking*

wagon, a once immaculate mother, five boys who had become thin and raggedy, and a girl who had matured beyond her years. She closed her diary, but not before first sniffing John's rosebud. She had looked for John and his golden chestnut mare whenever wagons drew near. She had shouted her name to passersby.

She felt the diary's leathery smoothness through cracked fingertips. The rosebud's scent brought back exquisite hours spent in the company of playing children and a laughing young man. Would she ever see John again? Or would she end up like those emigrants who had left behind dying oxen, personal treasures, heat-shrunk wagons, and loved ones? Would she wind up without a cross to mark her final resting place? Or would she be forced to join some Indian tribe and forget her Christian heritage?

Vienna watched the vermilion-painted Indians in a daze. She flinched at hearing Mother's voice.

"What are you seeing, daughter?"

"Red men—up there on that crag."

"Where?"

Vienna pointed. To her surprise, the Indians had vanished. Mother looked at her strangely. *Am I going mad?* Vienna asked herself. For weeks she had felt growing unrest. Facing the prospect of a premature death, she asked herself, *How do I get in God's good graces? How do I get that inner peace Mother spoke of?* The question kept her aflutter.

Am I in God's grace? she had asked herself the Sabbath day the tribe of friendly Crow veered off the trail. The question surfaced at Independence Rock near the Sweetwater River, where locusts devoured all vegetation and the first two oxen dropped from the yoke. It nagged in glaring alkali flats, where the cows and two more oxen starved to death. It nibbled in her mind as the family transferred their belongings to a lighter wagon that had been abandoned by some ill-fated family.

The question made her nerves snap as they toiled ever

higher to the South Pass of the Rocky Mountains. It sprang into focus under the merciless August sun as they plodded over the 50-mile stretch of grassless, waterless waste that struck due west from Sandy Creek to Green River, the cut-off Mother had chosen to save time.

And now, in Bear River country, disturbing smoke signals appeared on prominent peaks. Grim-faced Blackfoot Indians watched the wagon from surrounding hills. Elisha fell in with two trains that banded together for protection. The trains consisted of several companies. Vienna felt relief at seeing adult men with families. She hoped to meet girls her age.

A blond girl traveled two wagons ahead. She might be 15 or 16, though her straggly hair (she wore no bonnet) and her casual demeanor made her appear younger. Vienna tried to get acquainted, but the girl always seemed to be bantering with some young man who happened to ride beside her wagon.

Staying near her family, owing to the acute Indian danger, Vienna observed her fellow travelers. She'd always thought all families were alike, all mothers were alike, all brothers were alike. Not so! Some mothers complained and showed a temper. Some youngsters didn't do their chores as they were told. Some drivers rough-handled the oxen, something Elisha never did. Some youngsters carelessly walked over gravesites, apparently not realizing that human beings lay underneath. They didn't seem to care that death had separated families, and the same thing could happen to them. Vienna shuddered, thinking that some dead persons might have struggled alone when death overtook them.

She watched girls who talked saucily to young men, girls who talked of marriage and high hopes in the land of gold. Their mothers were pregnant women, women with babies and growing kids. The girls had fathers, Vienna noted, and the women had husbands. Some women came to the campfire and asked, "Where's your pa?"

"He's already in California," Vienna would answer. "He's making a home for us there. We don't have to start from scratch; Father has sent for us!"

Sometimes a woman replied, "You are so lucky." Other times, women merely exchanged glances and sighed.

It was after a noon stop that Vienna, mulling over the women's reactions, noticed that the train was catching up with a small company. The wagons had been waiting for the large train, and their leader asked permission to join up. Twenty-five wagons normally sufficed for defense, but these wagons were a mere remnant of a company. Permission granted, the wagons fell in line far ahead. The train was redivided into groups of 10 wagons each and travel resumed.

Vienna paid little attention to the incident. She was making entries in her diary. Suddenly, the blond girl's cackling laugh cut through the teamsters' commands and the monotonous grinding of the wheels. Stretching, Vienna saw a tall rider on a golden chestnut mare. He was bridling his mount, then turned and rode alongside the girl's seat.

John! It must be John! The shock of seeing her golden hero jolted Vienna. He hadn't seen her yet. Why wasn't he turning around? She waited impatiently for him to come her way. When he dashed off, forward, she felt abandoned and utterly wretched.

At corraling time she tried to spot his wagon. She saw him at one of the campfires—not alone, but in the company of the blond girl, a younger man, and two other girls. The blond girl's hair was brushed and the blouse she wore showed creases as though it had just been pulled from a trunk. Half woman, half child, she sported wet lips that parted quickly in John's presence. Her easy repartee left Vienna tongue-tied and helpless.

"Is anything amiss, daughter? Are you ill?" Mother felt Vienna's forehead.

"Nothing is amiss, Mother. I feel fine."

"Then why do you look so glum?" Elisha wanted to know.

"I don't know," Vienna snapped. "I've been sort of mad at everything lately." She wished everybody would leave her alone.

Chapter Eleven
Campfires

John rode in Vienna's direction the next morning, but he turned his mare and stopped three wagons ahead. Vienna jumped at seeing him. Why was he keeping company with that blond girl? What did that girl have that she, Vienna, lacked? Did she have business skills? Could she make a proper wife and partner for John? Vienna raged inside, only to admit to herself that the girl probably had everything—a mature body, communication skills, and everything else. Vienna looked at herself, feeling flat.

The rose in her diary—did it mean anything at all? Did young swains give rosebuds to girls without meaning their promises? Needing a place to hide, she took refuge in the wagon. She was sobbing uncontrollably when she heard John's voice.

"Mrs. Brooks, ma'am, how is Vienna?"

"My daughter is fine, thank you." Mother sounded cool.

"Has she spoken of me?" John asked.

"She has."

"Do you— Do you wish to tell me something, ma'am?" John sounded cautious.

"My daughter is too young, John. Come back two or

three years hence, and we shall discuss anything you have to say."

Vienna dried her tears—but not quickly enough, for John had dashed off when she emerged at the foremost hoop.

"How could you, Mother!" she accused. "Now he may never come back."

"He will if he is the solid person you say he is."

"But what if he changes his mind, what with all those—girls around?"

"Then you had best look for another man."

"I mustn't lose him, Mother! I love John." There. Her secret was out. The one she'd meant to keep forever.

Mother looked at her sharply. "Love is no guarantee for wedded bliss, daughter. Marriage is a working proposition. Many a girl has regretted her whirlwind courtship."

"But Mother, John will wait for me to grow up."

"Good. Then both of you have time to let your love mature." Mother's voice softened. "If you still feel the same a few years hence, your father and I will gladly give our blessing. Believe me, daughter, we want only your happiness."

Vienna turned away. *A few years* . . . Mother might as well have said a lifetime. While doing her chores during the noon stop, she listened to giggles and laughs coming from John's campfire. Normally a group-loving person, Vienna didn't feel like joining the older girls around John's fire. The girls cast flirtatious glances at John. Was John returning them? Vienna felt stabs of jealousy. There was no way she could go over and tell the girls that John was hers and hers alone.

She wished she knew how to play adult games. How did one compete with older girls for a man's attention? Mother, the schoolmaster, and the church elder had taught her many useful rules, but nothing she could apply to the present situation. She wished she could ask her Michigan friend for advice. Priscilla might know how to act, because her mother, unlike other frontier women, freely discussed men and romance with her daughter.

While Mother was visiting a sick lady at the next wagon and the little boys played safely in her vicinity, Vienna used the moment to flee the blond girl's cackling laughter. She took refuge behind a large rock and stared, unseeing, at canyon walls. Steps beside her made her spin around. *John!*

"You oughtn't to be out here all by yourself," he admonished. "Too dangerous." His voice was soft.

"Oh, John, I couldn't bear listening to that blond girl's laughter. Are you sweet on her?"

"Vienna!" he clucked. "Have you so little faith in me?"

"Why do you keep company with her?" Vienna challenged. "She's a tease and uses language like a teamster. She's a slouch, and probably has no business skills at all."

He laughed out lcud. "Jealous, my dear Vienna? Don't you know I've been looking for you? I saw your name on the markers you left by the road, and returning emigrants passed on your message. Now that I've found you, whenever I try to ride past that girl's wagon she stops me." He looked at Vienna tenderly. "No, no, my dear Vienna, that blond girl would never do." He sat down beside her. "We'll build our cabin in California, a fine house, maybe, with rooms for all of us. There'll be a room for you and me, another room for my brother, and a room for dear old Mother where she can go when her sick headaches come on. . . And there'll be a room for our children." He lifted her chin, smiling.

Vienna felt blissfully secure. "I wish you'd never leave me, John. I wish we could get married right away."

"Patience, my little rosebud!" He laid her head against his chest. She heard the strong and steady beat of his heart. His clothes smelled of herbs and fresh sage, a good smell. She snuggled close, knowing she'd cherish this moment forever.

"I love you, John," she whispered.

"I love you too, my darling wife-to-be." He gently drew her to her feet. "We must go back. This place is dangerous, and I wouldn't want anything bad to happen to you." Taking her hand in his, he continued, "You have told your mother about me."

She averted her eyes. "Yes."

"What did she say?"

"She wasn't very encouraging," Vienna hedged.

"I shall speak to her again," he stated. "We *can* wait until we get settled in California." He lifted her hand to his cheek. "I am so fortunate I found you in Kanesville the day you struggled against that brutal man."

Vienna shuddered. "Our *dear* teamster. He was like a creature from the underworld, devoid of light and decency. Hold me, John, so I shall never fear the likes of him again. How cruel and slimy he was! He stole our beans, and he made us suffer."

"It's all right," John comforted, "you're safe."

"I hate him, John."

"No, Vienna, you must forgive. It was he who brought us together." John guided her to the edge of the camp, then left.

Mother stood at the wagon, waiting. "Where have you been, daughter?"

"Not far, Mother."

"Have you seen John?"

"Only for a minute, Mother."

"Did he tell you about his family?"

"He travels with his mother and younger brother."

"What happened to his father?"

"I don't know, Mother. We never talked about that."

"Have you met his mother?"

"No, I haven't."

"How do you know what kind of person John is, not even knowing his family?"

"I just know, Mother."

"You know precious little about him."

"I know enough, Mother. John is a good man."

"Oh, Vienna, even the most capable girl can follow the wrong man and suffer her mistake for a lifetime."

Vienna kept silent for the sake of peace. Mother pointed to one of the wagons ahead. The blond girl was headed for John's wagon, carrying a steaming plate. "What do you make of this, daughter?"

"I, uh, don't know, Mother." Vienna felt a kick in her stomach. She herself had been thinking of meeting John's mother. But not once had John invited, "Meet dear old Mother." He hadn't had time to invite her to meet his family, she guessed.

The blond girl's hair was neatly tacked into a sun bonnet with not a wisp escaping. The fair face was scrubbed, and a clean dress replaced the grimy skirt and creased blouse she had worn earlier. Vienna watched with riveted attention. Why hadn't John invited her to meet his mother, instead of the girl who meant nothing to him?

> ### Flapjacks
> Warm milk and hot flapjacks made a wonderful breakfast. Even Justus and Elijah, fussy eaters ate with gusto.
>
> 1 cup milk
> ½ cup stoneground yellow cornmeal
> ½ cup flour
> ½ teaspoon salt
> 1 egg well beaten
>
> Combine all ingredients and stir until mixed. Drop by the spoonful onto a hot, greased griddle. Cook on one side until bubbles form, turn and cook on other side. Serve with maple syrup or molasses. (4 servings.)

Mother had impressed upon her since childhood that one graciously waited for an invitation—unless somebody was ill or needed help. Surely John must know that his future wife had learned those rules. Vienna watched the girl, regretting she had listened to her mother's advice.

The girl didn't pussyfoot around. She didn't call to make her presence known, either. Instead, she unhesitatingly climbed up and approached the canvas opening.

Vienna hung her head. Surely the girl had been invited. About to turn away in misery, Vienna uttered a gasp. A woman's shrill voice sounded from John's wagon. The girl came out in great haste. Bonnet askew, she scrambled from the wagon and beat a hasty retreat. The plate flew from her hands and food spilled in all directions. After the girl's hasty exit, Vienna fell into spells of silence. She worried that John's mother might not like her any better than she did the blond girl.

Toward evening, a woman up front began shrieking hysterically. Vienna raced ahead to see what had happened. The camp was in an uproar, and suddenly she saw why. In the deep canyon, shut in by sheer walls, she recoiled from the wreckage of a wagon train. Marks of an Indian attack—arrow-pierced canvas tops, overturned wagons, blood-crusted rags, robbed trunks, barrels, and boxes—shook her to the bone.

A headboard thrust into a fresh mound of earth told a tale of horror. The day before, the inscription explained, a company had found the wreckage and dead men stripped of clothing, scalped, and multilated and had buried the victims under this mound. No women or children were found.

Viewing with alarm an Indian fire on the cliff above, the emigrants cooked supper with portions of the wreck fueling their fires. Scouts rode ahead to find a safe location for the night. Leaders advised everybody to light bonfires and prepare to move.

Vienna was tossing wagon spokes into the fire when

the last scout returned. She didn't see him until he passed in the firelight. Straightening up, she noticed a chestnut mount and its tall rider. She knew only one rider who sat so tall in the saddle. "John!" she called, silly for joy. Soon now he'd turn and flash his white teeth in a huge smile! She chuckled. How surprised he'd be on seeing her!

"John!" she called again. When he still didn't turn around, she yelled, "BIG Z, wait for me!" She broke into a run, arms outstretched.

He heard her at last. Pulling up his horse, he half turned. "Are you calling me, Miss?"

The stranger's stare jolted Vienna. She had made a mistake. "I'm sorry," she stammered. "You reminded me of—somebody."

He tipped his hat. "No harm done, Miss."

Vienna's insides churned. If this man wasn't John, then where was John? Blinded by tears, she stumbled over rocks. John was dead, that's what. He had perished in this savage wilderness, pierced by Indian arrows—after some gruesome torture, perhaps. Some Indian had surely taken his scalp. Her imagination ran wild.

She tripped over an outcropping and fell screaming to the ground. What was the use of going on? Why drag things out when it was obvious they'd never reach that silly Sierra or the golden land Father had written about. Father! How could he send his family on a journey he knew so well held mortal dangers? How could he suggest they follow him?

"I hate you, Pa! Hate you, hate you, hate you!" Vienna's muffled screams drummed in her ears.

A hand kept her from crying out loud again. "Hush, child, hush." Mother's voice was gentle, but oh, so sad. Crickets chirped and frogs croaked. Had she gone mad? Vienna wondered.

"Where am I, Mother?"

"In the wagon by the river. You are safe, child."

"How did I get here?"

"A scout carried you back to us. Be still and drink." Mother eased soothing tea down Vienna's throat.

She drifted into fitful sleep. At sunrise she couldn't make herself get up. Between waking and sleeping she sipped the herbal tea Mother offered. Barely aware of the rumbling wagon, she couldn't say how many hours or days had passed since she collapsed by the fire.

Hate you! Hate you! Hate you! The words pounded in her head. Had she really spoken such outrageous words? Hate Father?

Chapter Twelve
Sierra-bound

As Vienna recovered from her fever at a place called Soda Springs, she noticed that many emigrants took a northerly direction, while Elisha aimed for the southwestward trail.

"Our protectors will make their homes in Oregon," Mother explained. She had been nursing Vienna with angelic devotion.

Vienna nodded. She climbed, jelly-legged, from the wagon and filled her cup with the bubbly water from the water casks. John's wagon was nowhere in sight, she noticed. Too weak to walk around, she returned to the wagon.

"I am sorry, Mother," she said in passing.

"About what, daughter?"

"About what I said." Vienna couldn't be more specific.

Mother gave her a tired smile. "You have been under some great strain, daughter."

By the end of the noon stop, Vienna managed to eat a bite. Sitting idly on the wagon, she watched the twins. She hadn't paid much attention to her brothers since the climb on Independence Rock, where she vainly hunted for John's name. She couldn't remember how many days, weeks, or miles ago that was, but she did recall that the boys had rejoiced on discovering Father's name. She hadn't exactly shared their ecstasy. For that matter, she hadn't contributed to the family's happinesss of late. She realized that, more often than not, she was grouchy and quick-tempered.

"Come under, Nig!" The twins, tottering under a yoke they couldn't carry, called the huge black ox. The animal lowered his head, allowing the boys to fasten the bow.

"Come under, Brock!" Old Brockle Face swung his long horns carefully under the yoke, following the twins' call.

"Come under, Nig! Come under, Brock. Whoa, haw!" A happy sound. Vienna had taken the call for granted, never giving it any thought. *How extraordinary my brothers are,* she mused. When the boys had turned 9, Father had given each twin a yearling calf. Vienna remembered how the twins had trained the young steers. Using rope harnesses, they rode astride the yearlings' backs and yoked them to their sleds and hauled the winter's wood. The animals did the twins' bidding, obedient as kittens. The oxen hadn't given the twins an ounce of trouble on the entire journey. Like family members, they had been pulling their share of the load. Sharp-ribbed and gaunt, they went under the yoke out of their own free will.

Mother lifted the yoke for the smaller oxen up front. Her body betraying strain, she nevertheless managed encouraging words for the twins and a hug for Justus, who did his level best to help. Vienna was amazed. How had she been so blind not to see how special her family was?

Resuming the journey, Vienna started the Lord's Prayer many times, then despaired over the part dealing with forgiveness. "I must forgive Pa," she mumbled. "I must forgive him and mean it." The thought accompanied Vienna north of the Great Salt Lake and westward to the Humboldt River. Trudging over barren mountains and burning deserts, she carried on a fierce inner struggle.

August drew into September. The mainstream of the 1852 emigration had passed. Late parties overtaking the

Brookses' wagon expressed fear of encountering early winter storms in the high Sierra, the last great barrier separating the weary travelers from California's sunland. Anxiety showed itself in the impatient manner people snapped at each other, and surfaced on Sabbath days when teamsters whipped draft animals while women read the Bible or sang hymns.

A few strangers stopped and offered sips of water along with kind words. Vienna prayed for the stragglers, and her own family, too. She dared not dwell on the family's dwindling food supplies or the empty water cask.

In the desert's stillness she perceived new thoughts. Had father suffered as much on his journey through the wilderness? Mother said he was not a well man. Was he worrying about his little girl, his sons, and Mother, who was risking everything in order to reunite the family? Had he taken ill on his journey, the same as she had a while back? Knowing the trail's dangers, was he agonizing over the fate of his family? If they failed to arrive, would he blame himself and be sorry forever? Vienna shuddered, knowing she wouldn't want to be in her father's shoes.

She watched gathering vultures and wondered about the carrion birds' next meal. A vulture was circling downwind from smelly carcasses and flew so low she could see his naked red neck. Wolves had torn apart the carcasses of two oxen and scattered the pieces. Trunks, boxes, and wagon parts lay about in reckless profusion, telling a tale of despair. Flies buzzed about and the stench of death was strong.

"Do you suppose—?" Vienna addressed Mother. She tied her sun bonnet tight, praying she'd never see human remains with missing scalps, or scalps hanging over some Indian wigwam, or, worse, lose her own scalp.

"Do not mourn for the people who abandoned these things, daughter; they are in God's hands," Mother told her.

During the night Vienna didn't dare fall asleep. Wolves approached the wagon, testing the oxen's mettle. Old Brock's long horns sent them into retreat. Brock hated wolves.

The war whoop of Shoshone Indians nearly stopped Vienna's heart. Their startling shrieks scared the oxen into a whirlwind stampede. Vienna felt her flesh crawl as she listened to the clatter of hooves.

"Old Brock! Old Nig!" Elisha's wail could have melted the starry host of the firmament. The frantic boy dashed after his pets the instant the sun's red hues colored the eastern horizon. He disappeared in no time on his Indian pony. Mother spent two days on bent knees praying for his safe return. Miraculously, with the help of men from a passing company, the 11-year-old retrieved the two black oxen.

The twins made night watch a habit and continued to hunt for feed. Anxiety over the oxen's health and safety showed on their faces. Earlier teams had clipped trailside pastures, forcing Nig and Brock to subsist on meager growth found in off-trail ravines and around hidden springs.

The Humboldt, a snaking desert river (in present-day Nevada), sustained the oxen from crossing to crossing. Vienna plodded in the powder-dry part of the riverbed. Grass along the banks crumbled under Mother's feet, breaking the desert's silence. The river's hot and bitter water threatened to vanish altogether at a place called Humboldt Sink.

In late September, 300 miles from the Brookses destination, the wagon came to a creaking halt. Fatigue etched each face as the family went about their evening chores. Mother scraped the last cup of flour from the barrel and made flapjacks. Vienna and her brothers stood around the fire, solemnly waiting for their last meal.

"I'll never forgive our teamster for stealing our beans," Elisha spat out.

Mother shook the smoking skillet. "No, Elisha, remember our Lord who forgave His tormentors. Forgive, and you will be forgiven."

"Sorry, Mother, I forgot." The boy's brows relaxed.

Was it coincidence that Mother glanced at Vienna? the girl wondered.

Mother blessed the food. "May the Lord send His ravens to provide the next meals for you, my children." She handed out the leathery flapjacks.

Vienna chewed and rechewed, savoring the sweet aftertaste with deep appreciation. A yellow moon rose, bathing the desert in unearthly light. Justus crouched close, and she felt his shivering body. Mother enfolded Elmont and Orion in her arms. She started to pray:

"Dare to do right,
Dare to be true!
Keep the great Judgment Day always in view.
Look at your work as you'll look at it then,
Scann'd by Jehovah, and angels, and men."

Vienna sensed Mother's gaze. Was the prayer meant for her? Mother rarely scolded, showing instead by example how to do a thing and do it right. Though strict at times, Mother was fair. Was she more concerned about her only daughter than about her five boys? The question nagged Vienna. Mother usually was cheerful, correcting with a laugh or a merry twinkle. Not this time!

During the family's Sabbath services, Vienna noticed Mother's subtle references to God's commandment, "Honour thy father." Vienna had carefully avoided Mother's hints, not allowing herself to get upset or sick again. Nevertheless, she grappled with herself. Was she guilty of breaking God's law? If God called her away, would she be acceptable to Him? Would she be saved?

In their bed under the wagon, Vienna hugged her mother. "I love you, Mother. I wouldn't do anything to hurt you—or Pa."

Mother returned Vienna's squeeze with unexpected vehemence. Turning on her side, Vienna sensed soft rocking motions in the bony body beside her. Was Mother weeping? A huge lump exploded inside Vienna. Hot tears rushed to her eyes and suddenly her cheeks felt wet.

"Help me to forgive Pa; please *help me,* dear Lord," she sobbed.

Chapter Thirteen
A Man on a Mule

While the twins cut rushes for the oxen the next morning, Vienna made final entries in her diary. In the course of her family's 2,500-mile journey she had collected facts and observations that might be useful to people who found her journal. She expressed hope that the finder would inform her father about what had happened to Eliza Ann Brooks and her six children. She added a last line: *PS: I love you, Pa. Please forgive any resentment I may have held against you for a while.*

She inhaled once more the fragrance of John's rosebud. Whatever had happened to John, wherever he might be, he was in God's good hands. On the page facing the rose she wrote *All is well.*

Vienna put the diary away. The disturbing inner voice was silenced, leaving peace in its place. She had quit judging. Troublesome images no longer tormented her mind. As she prayed the Lord's Prayer without stumbling, she knew that true peace comes through forgiveness, grace through love.

Bending over the river, she closed her eyes to the decaying carcasses and rusting wagon wheel rims staring at her through the slimy surface. She brushed away the scum and lapped up the bitter liquid. The oxen snorted at the smelly water, then drew it up in thirsty gulps. Later, they dozed in the water, their bony bodies partially submerged, refusing to eat until their hides absorbed some moisture.

While Elisha insisted on cutting more rushes, she and Elijah took turns in filling the water cask. The younger boys were chasing grasshoppers, and judging by their grave faces Vienna knew they were not playing. Grasshoppers were a common Indian food. Hungry as she was, she had no curiosity to find out what the long-legged insects might taste like.

But her little brothers didn't eat the grasshoppers they caught. They used them for bait on pin hooks and caught some small fish. Mother fried their catch in a smoking, greaseless pan.

"I have prayed to the Lord that He may provide for you, my children. May He forgive us for killing these poor little fish," she said sadly.

"Come under, Nig! Come under, Brock!"

The oxen merely rolled their eyes in acknowledgment of the twins' call. Saliva drooled from their open mouths like glistening veils. The wheels rolled on, propelled by their owners' need to get closer to their promised land. The shimmering-white desert stretched from one barren mountain to another. Vienna yearned for the sight of green . . . She felt lucid and light. A lake appeared in the distance. Gently waving plants bordered limpid waters reflecting a city of palaces, columns, spires, and domes. *Jerusalem?* She pushed through the hot sand, impatient to reach that wonderful city.

Elisha's yell dispelled her mirage. "Pa! It's our pa!"

Vienna's shimmering vision burst like a soap bubble. Where it had been, a horseback rider appeared— No, it was a man astride a mule, a wayworn traveler like themselves. Something familiar about his form made her rush forward. Joyfully, she fell into her father's arms. Then they

106

all hugged and kissed, crazy with joy and utter relief.

Mother's greeting was jubilant. "The children are all here, see?" She lined up Vienna and the boys. Elisha and Elijah, Justus, Orion, and little Elmont stood like wobbly organ pipes. Vienna couldn't miss her father's wet eyes as he contemplated the skinny, sun-darkened, ragged youngsters in front of him.

He looked around. "Where is your teamster?"

"We don't have one!" Elisha blurted. "Jeffrey deserted at the Missouri River, and Red stole our beans on the Fourth of July. We've been doing the driving ourselves, me and Elijah."

Shock registered on Father's sharp features. "I feared the worst," he confessed. "Your mother's letter from the States took four months to reach the mines. I set out in all haste to find my family. Riding from wagon to wagon, I inquired about you. Ten days ago a party recalled a girl

Bean Soup

"Eat, children, dinner is ready!" Mother served the plump, steaming beans in battered tin bowls. The skins were peeling, exposing the starchy insides. After the blessing, the family ate their first real meal together in two and a half years.

3 cups navy, pea, or little white beans
1 teaspoon baking soda
¼ cup molasses

optional:
3 small onions, cut in chunks
2 green peppers, cut in strips

The night before cooking, put beans to soak in kettle and cover with water. The next morning, change the water and simmer for 5 minutes. Stir in soda and watch it fizz. Continue to simmer for about 40 minutes, then test for tenderness: when skins of two beans crack when you blow on them, they are done.

Pour the cloudy, yellowish liquid off the tender beans and cover with 5 cups fresh water. Return to heat to simmer for about 30 more minutes.

(6 generous servings)

who seemed anxious to pass on a message. Somebody recalled her name—'Vienna, like the city in Austria.'"

Vienna's hand flew to her mouth. She had left her message for John.

Father opened his saddlebags and the family crowded around him.

"Beans and hardtack!" the boys cried.

They pressed against Father in the wagon's meager shade. The boys fell over the hardtack, chattering like squirrels. Vienna was too excited to eat. She studied Father. His blond hair had darkened, he had grown a beard, and he was shorter than she remembered. His stocky build was unchanged, though he had lost weight and his posture betrayed fatigue.

"Are you well, Pa?" she worried aloud.

"Never better!" He held her at arm's length, smiling. "My little girl has grown up."

Turning to Mother he said, "We mustn't delay our journey, for we are up against weeks of strenuous travel. We shall hitch my mule and your pony in front of the oxen and, God willing, reach Bidwell Bar by way of Jim's new pass."

"Who is Jim?" Mother asked.

"James Pierson Beckwourth to most people; Jim to us local folk," Father explained. "Jim opened a pass that is some 2,000 feet lower than Donner Pass and considerably easier to negotiate."

Loose hair softened the fine new lines in Mother's sun-darkened face. The corners of her mouth tilted upward in a smile. "You saved us from the clutches of famine, dearest."

He put his arm around her thin waist. "Your journey required a stout heart. How did you ever manage?"

"I remembered Lot's wife, dearest. I didn't dare look back. We started out with eight oxen and two milk cows. Our animals dropped by the wayside, one by one."

Elisha quit munching. He looked shamefaced. "I'm sorry, Mother."

"It wasn't your fault," Mother assured him. "You did well."

"We did save the oxen you gave us, Pa," Elisha defended himself.

Father laid a hand on the boy's shoulder. "You mean these gaunt longhorns are Old Brock and Old Nig?"

Elisha nodded vigorously.

Mother's eyes grew wet. "Elisha always managed to find feed and water for his pets, and he taught his twin how to care for the animals. Elijah has learned so much, and he is more courageous than ever—thanks to his brother."

Father clucked. "Elisha always has been a spunky lad. Glad to hear his twin is getting to be more like him."

Vienna snuggled up to Father as the family got reacquainted and caught up on news. Father warned of a long, hot drive ahead. He spoke of a sawmill at a place called Berry Creek, where he and three millhands had stored the lumber he planned to sell at dear prices in the spring.

"And where will we live?" Vienna asked.

"In a vacated miner's cabin, kitten. The Bidwell cabin will be our winter home. In the spring we shall look for a place suitable for a dairy business."

"I can't wait, Pa." Vienna snuggled against her father, feeling warm and safe.

"For now, we must travel to a river called Truckee." Father's voice weakened as he spoke. Sweaty beads collected on his forehead.

Mother's face dimmed with concern. "Are you all right, dearest?"

"How could I not be all right, having found my family alive and well?"

Despite her father's smile, Vienna didn't like his sudden flush.

"We had better move on," Father urged. "There are still 300 tough miles ahead." He harnessed his mule and Elisha's Indian pony in front of the oxen and started to walk beside the wagon. His gait soon became unsteady. Suddenly he keeled over.

"Quick, Mother!" Vienna cried as she ran to her father's side.

They helped him to the wagon and lifted him inside. Mother looked pale.

"The long ride was too much for your father. We must nurse him back to health." Loosening his clothes, Mother covered him with a light blanket. Climbing from the wagon, she turned to the twins. "Do you think you can handle the mule?"

"Yes, Mother." Elisha elbowed his twin.

"Y-yes, Mother," Elijah added.

The twins outdid each other driving the team. After sunset they rested and cooled off.

Father gave directions and advice. "After passing the Humboldt Sink, where the river loses itself into the ground, we shall drive through 40 miles of dry desert," he informed the family. "There will be no water except for some boiling springs halfway across."

"Can we make the springs if we travel by night?" Elisha asked. "We traveled by night before."

Father grasped Elisha's hand. "I was about to recommend a night march. I am proud of you, son. You have taken to the trail like a man."

Elisha's smile made Vienna realize that she had never seen her brother so happy.

At their last camping place before the waterless desert they filled cask, keg, jugs, canteens, teakettle, and other containers with water and cut extra rushes for the oxen. Mother soaked the beans Father had brought in the pail that hung under the wagon.

They had sustained themselves on hardtack since meeting Father. The bad river water they drank then swelled the bread and caused stomach cramps. Even so, the hungry feeling had been worse. Vienna suffered in silence, but she so looked forward to a hot meal.

After a grueling two-day march, they reached the boiling springs Father had mentioned—a circular area encrusted with lava that held several springs. Large gushers spouted tall columns of steam, and little ones fell back into their own bubbly basins. Vienna held her nose against the unpleasant fumes that smelled like rotten eggs.

Mother carried the bean kettle to a small spring. Her footsteps sounded as if she were walking on hollow clay. She vanished into the wafting vapor clouds, then stepped back quickly. "Watch yourselves, children," she warned. "This area is dangerous. People and animals have perished in these pools." She kept the younger boys away from the killer springs and soothed Elmont, who started to scream. "Hush, everything is all right."

Elisha and Vienna ventured into the steam several times and dipped the bucket into the rapidly boiling water. Back at the wagon they poured the foaming liquid into pans. Mother, Elijah, and Justus struggled to hold back the thirsty animals. Waiting for the water to cool, Vienna listened to the springs' odd gurgling and rumbling sounds. The place was positively eerie.

Elisha nudged her. "We're lucky we can cook our beans, Sis. There isn't a thing around here we can use for lighting a fire."

Vienna nodded. "It's amazing how the Lord has always provided some sort of fuel along the way—buffalo chips, dry weeds, abandoned wagons, and now boiling springs. God cared for us in the same way He cared for the children of Israel on their journey through the wilderness."

She dipped her hand into the pans. The water felt lukewarm to the touch. Shoving a pan in front of Old Brock she urged, "Come on, have some. This may be the last time you'll drink desert water."

When the ox guzzled, she saw that the mule stuck his

head into Elisha's pan, then pulled it out, braying. Elisha grinned. "So you don't like mineral water, huh? Well, you've got a lot to learn." Elisha swished the clear water until the mule started to sip.

Vienna heaved a sigh of relief. Without drinking, the animals would not eat. Without eating, they'd be too weak for the long haul to the Truckee, the mountain stream Father had talked about.

"Eat children, dinner is ready!" Mother served the plump, steaming beans in battered tin bowls. The skins were peeling, exposing the white, starchy insides. After the blessing, the family ate their first real meal together in two and a half years. Father barely touched his food. Weak with fever, he returned to his bed in the wagon.

Vienna filled all their containers with hot springwater, and the boys fed the animals from the dried rushes stored in the wagon. While the oxen chewed their cuds, the family rested. Refreshed, they struck out at dusk to cross the last stretch of desert.

Chapter Fourteen
The New Pass

Dusk cooled the burning desert sand, and the cold
night air made traveling easier. Vienna looked skyward.
How clear and bright the midnight stars looked!

She faced the journey's rough reality when the wagon
creaked to a halt at a large sand dune. Without being told,
she took her stand at the left front wheel. Mother put her
shoulder to the wheel behind her and the twins toiled at
the opposite side. The younger boys pushed and pulled,
while oxen, mule, and pony struggled for footing. Slowly,
the wagon pulled forward.

Partway across the dune, Elisha rested the animals.
Sweat drenched the mule's hide. "I guess he isn't used to
pulling a wagon," Elisha remarked. He unhitched the mule
and let him roll in the sand.

After their brief rest, the family struggled onward. Yard
by yard, they conquered the dune. The night wind blew
fine sand into their faces; the needlelike grains pricked
Vienna's skin. Prairie wolves (Father called them coyotes)
yipped in the wee hours, and still the family pressed on.

Brief rests, water, and a little feed kept the draft animals
going. By sunrise their pace had slackened to a crawl. The

moment the wagon stopped Vienna poured the last trickle of water from the barrel. Mother and the twins lifted the yoke, freeing the oxen.

While the mule rolled in the sand and Elisha rubbed down his pony, Vienna offered the water to the oxen. Her calloused hand stroked the animals' rough hides, feeling the sharp, protruding ribs. She spoke gentle words.

Yoked once more in front of the wagon, the oxen pulled with what appeared to be their last strength. Vienna watched their drooling, wide-open mouths with mounting horror. The oxen were like members of the family; they mustn't lose these faithful friends.

"Old Brock, Old Nig, please keep going," she rasped, herself thirsty and exhausted.

The oxen didn't so much as glance sideways. Gaunt and tottering, they labored under the heavy yoke.

Elisha's yell rent the air. "Trees, I can see trees! There's a river ahead!"

Following the boy's lusty cry, the mule took off with breakneck speed, forcing pony, oxen, and wagon to follow.

"Wait, not so fast! Do you want to kill us?" Elisha shouted.

The oxen sniffed and kept up with the runaway mule. Their staggering run filled Vienna with dismay. "Hold them back, Elisha!" she cried.

Mother raised her voice. "No, Elisha, they smell water! Let them go lest they trample you to death."

Elisha jumped aside not a second too soon.

Running behind the bucking wagon, Vienna remembered Father. "Pa, get off the wagon!" she cried.

Father jumped off near the riverbank just before mule, pony, and oxen plunged into the mountain stream's swift current. Fortunately, the wagon didn't turn over. Seeing the upright wagon and her father's ashen face, Vienna dropped to her knees and joined Mother in a song of thanks.

Then Mother rose and straightened her dress. "I didn't

think the oxen had that much spunk left," she remarked.

They hauled the wagon out of the riverbed and freed the draft animals, letting them drink and soak to their heart's content. Gladness replaced Vienna's anxiety as she washed off dust and grime.

Mother scrubbed her arms, face, and neck before swishing sweaty clothes in the cool water. "Let us wash the journey's dust from our travel-stained garments and way-worn bodies," she encouraged.

"Is the wilderness behind us, Mother?" Vienna asked.

"Yes, daughter. Only the Sierra Nevada separates us from our Promised Land."

Happiness rippled through Vienna as they pitched camp under cottonwood trees that lined the Truckee's riverbed. She helped Mother cook and wash and mend clothes. The twins fixed harnesses and wagon spokes, preparing for the final leg of the journey.

Elisha called, "Do we have any rags left, Mother?"

Mother looked up from the button she was sewing on a boy's faded shirt. She cut off the thread. "Do you need them for the wheels, son?"

"Yes, Mother, the iron tires are coming loose."

Mother climbed in the wagon and returned with a bolt of cloth. "Use this, son."

Vienna was aghast. "Mother, we saved the fabric to sew new clothes."

Mother tossed the bolt to Elisha. "We shall sew no clothes if we don't get to California, daughter."

The twins unrolled the material, then wound the cloth around the wheels to hold them together. Tears stung Vienna's eyes. How much more must they sacrifice?

Before them lay the new pass so much praised by Father, a gateway provided for the purpose of saving the family of Eliza Ann Brooks. No, Vienna corrected herself, the family of George Washington Brooks.

Mountain peaks 7,000 feet high hid in gathering clouds.

Was John up there right now, or had he already descended? She sensed that he was alive. "Someday I'll see him again," she whispered to herself.

"How long until we get to California?" the boys pestered Father.

"Two, three weeks, if everything goes well," Father answered.

A bank of white cumulus clouds rose from the horizon at dawn. Within hours, the clouds covered the sky like a giant white tent. Warm raindrops fell on Vienna's face. She licked them off her cracked lips and let the rest evaporate.

Mother cast concerned looks skyward. "Autumn is catching up with us," she said. "Before long, it will be winter."

Autumn or not, they traveled on in 90 degree heat. Vienna pulled down her bonnet, shielding her eyes against the bright glare. She wished Father's health hadn't broken down. The mountains ahead looked formidable. The sky-high barrier challenged the courage of strong and healthy men. What if the team or wagon failed? What if their youthful teamsters couldn't manage? What if an early storm buried them in snow? Vienna's lips moved in silent prayer.

They negotiated three fordings of the Truckee's rocky riverbed and ascended the Sierra mountain chain. Following Father's directions, Elisha took the northern route by which they could reach the upper end of the Feather River canyon. They continued to unload heavy objects until the wagon contained little more than clothing and bedding. The last barrel rolled downhill while they ascended the Sierra, near the new pass. At Father's insistence, they kept the wagon jack.

The nights put frost on the ground. Vienna and Mother pulled a woolen blanket about themselves underneath the wagon. Vienna felt half-frozen after the great desert heat she had endured. On cold mornings she shrugged into her wool shawl.

The road was rough, but grass and wood were abundant. Birds called in evergreen trees and a few flowers still bloomed in sheltered places. Vienna could hardly believe her ears when Father said they had passed the summit and were descending into Jim's valley! Knowing herself to be on the western slope, she felt like singing.

Late berries remaining on creekside bushes tasted sweet as honey. Pines and cedars provided shelter against the October wind. Deer watched the wagon with pricked ears and liquid eyes. A doe stamped her feet, and a buck threw back shining antlers and bounded off in giant leaps. On an opposite slope, a herd of antelope dashed about. The animals' antics put smiles on Mother's face and triggered excited exclamations from Vienna's brothers.

Elisha shaded his eyes. What did he see this time? Vienna wondered. Leave it to Elisha's eagle eye to spot something unusual! "A house! There's a house down yonder!" Elisha yelled.

"There isn't any house around here," Vienna countered.

Elisha pointed. "There is too!"

Father stuck his head out of the foremost hoop. "Do you hear dogs barking?" he asked.

"They're at that house down there," Elisha said.

"Jim's house," Father confirmed.

"We haven't seen a house since Council Bluffs on the Missouri," Vienna told Father. "I didn't think we'd ever see an honest-to-goodness house again."

"I told you it was a house," Elisha said, looking satisfied.

Dogs soon surrounded the wagon in front of the house. A powerfully built man called them away. Standing in the doorway, he presented a strange picture. He was a dark-skinned man with long, braided hair reaching to his shoulders. Dressed in buckskin, with moccasins on his feet, he resembled an Indian.

"So you found your family, George," Jim addressed Father without formalities. To mother, he spoke courteously. "I am the proprietor of this valley, ma'am. Welcome to my ranch."

Jim's voice sounded strong and masterful, yet pleasant to the ear, Vienna thought. Without waiting for replies, Jim took sweetmeats from his pockets and distributed them among the youngsters. Tears reddened his eyes at seeing Elmont. "Poor little one, what a rough time you must have had! Do you want to ride on my horse? Do you want to have some fun?" Jim reached for the boy, but Elmont ran off screaming.

"The child is afraid of strangers," Mother apologized.

"Nobody needs to be afraid in my valley." Jim smilingly lifted the boy in his arms and stilled his crying with sweets from his pocket. Vienna couldn't believe her eyes—Elmont stroked the man's curly goatee!

Orion butted in. "I'll ride on your horse, if you'll let me—please!"

Jim handed Elmont back to his mother. To Vienna's astonishment, he fetched a horse that was half-saddled, just as Indians rode. Lifting Orion on top, he mounted the

Hardtack

Father opened his saddle bags and the family crowded around him. "Beans and hardtack!" the boys cried, falling on the hardtack, chattering like squirrels.

3+ cups white flour, unbleached all-purpose
1 tablespoon salt
1 cup water

Preheat the oven to 375°F. In a 2 quart bowl, mix the flour with the salt. Add the water and stir until mixture becomes too difficult. Knead dough in bowl with hand, adding more flour to make it very dry.

Press, pull, and use a rolling pin to roll the dough into a rectangle that can be divided into 3-inch squares of ½-inch thickness. Use a table knife to cut dough into squares. Holding each square in hand, punch 16 holes through it with an eight-penny nail, being careful not to hurt yourself.

Place dough squares in ungreased baking sheets and bake for 30 minutes, until crisp and lightly browned. Cool before storing in a closed container. (16 pieces)

horse behind the 6-year-old and took him for a fast ride. Vienna's chewy tidbit tasted like sweet, dried berries. She munched with pleasure, remembering a certain young man who had taken her brother for a ride back at the Platte River. Without being told, she helped Mother with chores. The twins chattered excitedly as they freed the draft animals to let them graze.

Invited into the house, the family warmed themselves by the fire and sat down to a hearty meal. Vienna had missed bread more than anything. She accepted her slice with expressions of gratitude. Along with cabbage, turnips, and radishes from Jim's kitchen garden, the bread turned the meal into a feast for kings.

Jim was not a young man anymore—older than Father, about 50, Vienna guessed. She couldn't take her eyes off his strange, dark features. His face spoke of kindness and of suffering. His voice spoke of amazing adventures. The former mountain man and trailblazer used to live with the Indians, Vienna learned. Because of his bravery he had become chief of the Crow. Jim's tales of Indian customs and of a grizzly bear fight left the entire family spellbound.

"Why don't you tell us how you discovered the new pass?" Father prompted.

Jim smiled. "Last year, while searching for gold, I entered an extensive valley at the northwest extremity of the Sierra Range," Jim recalled. "Swarms of wild geese and ducks were swimming on the surface of a cool, crystal stream that was the central fork of the *Rio de las Plumas.* My party and I struck out across this beautiful valley to the Yuba River and from there to the Truckee, which flowed east, telling us we were on the eastern slope of the mountain range."

Elisha leaned forward. "And then?"

"Wagon trains were coming west from the States," Jim continued. "I asked myself, 'How many parties will get caught in Sierra blizzards at the end of the trek? How many people will suffer? How many children will die?' The new pass, being gentler and lower, made disassembly or lowering of wagons by rope unnecessary."

"And then?" Elisha urged.

"Forgetting about gold, I turned back and urged people at the American Valley, Bidwell's Bar, and Marysville to build a wagon road." Jim flashed a broad smile. "It was my pleasure to lead the first party of 17 wagons safely over the pass. Wanting to help the emigrants coming this way, I established myself near the pass last spring.

"My house is the emigrants' landing place." Jim spoke with pride. "It is the first ranch they see in the Golden State, and the only house between here and Salt Lake."

Vienna could have listened to Jim Beckwourth forever. Their hospitable host was a hero the family would never forget. Vienna hated to leave. Back at the wagon, she questioned Father about their colorful benefactor.

"Mysteries too numerous to mention surround Jim," Father hedged. "Miners tell tall stories about Jim. Some say he's the son of a Black slave and a gentleman plantation owner in Virginia."

"He does speak like an educated man," Vienna interrupted. "How did he come to live here?"

"Miners say he came West as a fur trader and trailblazer, maybe even a soldier," Father continued. "They talk about his 10,000 adventures. Whatever and whoever Jim is, one thing is certain: he saved uncounted pioneers from a snowy Sierra grave." Father took a deep breath before climbing up into the wagon. "Without Jim's pass, we ourselves might be lost under the Sierra's snowy sheet."

"We must include Jim in our prayers," Vienna offered.

Father nodded. "God bless Jim and all the good people who assisted Mother and you children during your long journey. Now let us move on! There's a rocky road ahead."

Chapter Fifteen
Outrunning the Storm

After grazing in Jim's lush, clover-studded valley, the draft animals pulled with renewed vigor. Father had also benefited from the food and rest. He sat on the buckboard, directing Elisha, who held the reins.

They climbed over breathtaking mountain ridges, wending their way through rocky canyons and plunging down steep cliffs. The wagon, though mended and shrunken, held together as if by a miracle. Rough-locking of wheels, chaining logs to axletrees, and other measures to hold back the wagon challenged the young teamsters.

Through all their difficulties, Father insisted that the Feather River route was child's play compared to Donner Pass, the route most emigrants had taken. The toil of mountain travel etched new lines into Mother's face. Vienna resolved to help Mother all she could in California so that she could recover her strength.

Suddenly, on a windswept ridge, a stunning view unfolded before them. A great valley, golden with sunshine, stretched away into the distance. Elisha stopped the team.

Vienna's heart beat like a sledgehammer. "Look at this, Pa!" she called back into the wagon.

"Yup! It's California, your new home," Father confirmed. His voice rose to a higher pitch. "You are looking at the valley of the Sacramento, inhabited by Indians until recently. Captain Sutter opened the valley to people from the States. The nuggets that started the great gold rush and brought men like me to California were found on his property."

Vienna's heart pounded in her throat. "Where is Sutter's Fort, Pa?"

"You cannot see it from here. Why do you ask?"

"Emigrants who took the other route said they'll stop at Sutter's Fort. Can they do that, Pa?"

"Yes, kitten."

"Is Sutter's Fort far from Bidwell Bar?" Vienna ventured.

"Not as the crow flies. Traveling there is another matter, however. Why do you ask these questions?"

"Just curious." Vienna wanted to talk about John, but Father might not understand. The prospect of reaching their new home and meeting John again someday made her feel like singing.

Father ended Vienna's admiration of the golden valley beyond. Frowning at gray clouds racing over high peaks he said, "It's still Indian Summer in the valley, but those clouds are signaling the start of winter. There's going to be rain and lots of it."

"And up here?" Vienna hated herself for asking, for she knew the answer.

"We had better hasten on lest we get buried in 20 feet of snow," Father warned.

"Can't we stay a little while longer, Pa?" Vienna begged.

"No, kitten."

One cold morning Mother handed up the younger boys to Father and boosted herself onto the wagon. Vienna rode up front with the twins, resting her sore feet. The wagon jolted over the road that connected the high country with Bidwell Bar. Elisha drove the team, not an easy task on the washed-out, rutted road. Rocks under the animals' feet were foot-defying indeed.

Vienna listened to the *thump, thump, thump* of flattened wheels as they traveled along a wild mountain stream. She felt growing excitement. Another day and they'd arrive at what Father called "the end of the rainbow."

Sitting high on the wagon, Elisha threw off the blanket Mother had draped about his shoulders. "I don't need this; I'm warm enough," he boasted.

"You'll be glad you have the warm blanket in your tent tonight," Vienna admonished. "Father says this will be our last night under the stars."

"You mean under the clouds." Elisha caught a few whirling snowflakes that melted quickly on his hand.

Vienna tried hard not to think of the weather. The family had been running before the first storm of the season for two straight days. The trail that wound past tangled bushes and moss-covered rocks still had a summery feeling. Foliage did not yet display the deep reds and golds of a Michigan autumn. She ducked under green branches that brushed against the canvas roof behind her. Water sounds droned in her ears as she dreamed of John, her golden hero.

Suddenly she screamed and slammed into Elijah, who sat beside her. The wagon lurched and listed to one side. A wheel hit a rut and fell off the wagon.

Elisha struggled to hold back the team. "Whoa!"

Father parted the canvas. "Not another delay!" he moaned.

Elisha secured the brake and, looking shaken, fastened the reins before jumping off ahead of Elijah and Vienna. Retrieving the wayward wheel, jacking up the axle, and putting the wheel back in place proved an undertaking that required the combined efforts of the entire family. Time passed, and they still weren't able to travel on. Elisha rummaged through the toolbox and lifted out pincers, thongs, handfuls of nails and other hardware they had saved.

"What's wrong now?" Vienna fretted.

"We haven't got a spare linchpin left." Lips trembling, the young teamster turned to his mother. "We can't go on, Mother. What can we do?"

Mother gently nudged the boy. "Why don't you ask your father?" she encouraged.

Elisha tossed the hardware back into the toolbox with words that expressed his desperation. Vienna hoped he wasn't going to break down and cry. The immensity of her brother's responsibility and his small-boy size hit her like the sharp blow of a hammer.

"Go ask Pa!" she urged.

"We, uh, always managed before." Elisha drew a sleeve across his face.

Father, resting on a rock, asked for tools and a solid branch cut from a tree. With deft hands, he fashioned a wooden linchpin to replace the iron one they had lost. This will hold the wheel," he promised. "It's only pine, but it should last a while. Hickory would be better, but we haven't got any."

The delay proved to be costly. When darkness settled under giant pines in the primeval forest they were passing through, Father steered the team to a clearing. "You boys had best build a big campfire," he directed. "A roaring fire will keep the wolves and grizzlies away."

Grizzlies? As they lay by a great campfire that night Vienna worried about the great beasts. Shrieking winds echoed and reechoed from the mountains, and she heard snuffling sounds outside. Wolves growled and Old Brock pawed the ground, snorting.

Dawn's first gray light found Brock going wild. Vienna's knees shook the moment she left her bed underneath the wagon, and her throat knotted up. Among tree stumps and fallen branches she saw wolves divested of all hair except on the extremity of their noses, ears, and tails. Skeletons of oxen and bones, picked clean, were strewn about the clearing. Ravens and magpies fluttered noisily over the shaggy body of a bear.

The wolves, whose bodies were as bare as the palm of a hand, tore into the bear's belly. Growling, snapping, and baring their fangs, they yielded to the wrath of Elisha's ox. Muzzles dripping with blood, they retreated into the pines, then returned in greater numbers to attack the long-horned ox.

"Brock!" Elisha jumped into the middle of the fray. Wielding his whip, he lashed out at the wolves. "Don't you dare hurt my Brock!" he screamed.

The frantic young teamster and an ox gone mad forbade further traveling. Father sat glumly on a rock. Mother stoked last night's ashes, speaking soothing words. "This is not the end of the world, dearest. Brock will calm down and we shall continue our journey."

"You don't understand," Father worried. "We must outrun the storm. We simply must reach Bidwell Bar before nightfall."

"How far must we travel?" Mother inquired.

"Some 12 miles. We'll be there today if we hurry. Think about it—today!" Father brightened. "Perhaps we can travel without the oxen. The mule and pony might do. The wagon is light, and it's downhill all the way."

Mother's hand darted to her mouth. "Leaving our faithful oxen would be vicious indeed."

"The oxen may soon die anyway. Look at them! After all the poisonous water they drank on the trail they cannot last much longer. Their contaminated flesh will poison any animals that feed on them. After all, there isn't a hair left on these wolves."

Mother blanched. "We shan't leave without the twins' pets. We shan't hurt our boys."

Vienna had been watching and listening. She didn't know what else to do. Seeing Mother distraught tied her stomach into knots. Never before had Mother made a decision contrary to Father's wishes! If only Elisha and the ox settled down everything would be all right, she reasoned.

She picked up a large branch and joined Elisha in thrashing the dancing, saliva-drooling wolves. At last the wolves slunk away, leaving the bear to the screeching birds. But Brock would not go under the yoke! Much as they tried, the ox refused to cooperate. To make matters worse, the storm caught up with them. Snowflakes no longer melted. Footsteps left dark outlines on the white ground. Father hitched the mule and pony to the wagon.

"What are you doing, Pa?" Elisha cried.

Father pressed his hat down in his face. "Just over that rise is the Berry Creek sawmill I told you about. We can get there if we hurry."

"But Pa, what about Nig and Brock?"

"Your pets can roam free, son. They will not be far from you boys. We'll only stay at the mill until the storm blows over. We'll continue on to Bidwell Bar as soon as the weather clears up."

"But Pa, the wolves will drive Old Brock crazy."

Father ran a weary hand over his beard. "That's good, son. He will drive the critters away."

Elijah butted in. "Please don't leave our oxen behind, Pa! Please don't! They pulled us all the way from Michigan and never gave us any trouble."

"We're not abandoning the oxen, son. They can follow us to the mill."

The wind began tearing the canvas roof to tatters. Mother coaxed the weeping boys onto the wagon. Father cracked the whip. Mule and pony leaned forward in their harnesses and the wheels turned. Father urged the animals to hurry, and they headed for the rise. Vienna sobbed into her apron. She couldn't stand the oxen's bellowing.

Mother attempted to comfort the boys. "Old Brock and Old Nig will be safe," she stressed. "They'll follow us before long."

The boys' loud weeping made it plain that they would not be comforted.

Mother coaxed Vienna, "Why don't you record this day in your diary, daughter. We must not forget this important day."

Vienna sniffled. "What do you want me to record?"

"The end of our journey, daughter." Mother put on a cheerful smile.

"What's so great about today?" Vienna wiped the backs of her hands over eyes and cheeks, drying her tears.

"Today, October 28, 1852, exactly six months after our departure, we are reaching the sawmill in Berry Creek in Butte County, California, where your father has spent two years cutting lumber and preparing for our future home."

"Our journey is not finished yet, Mother." Vienna didn't feel like writing. A glance through the small round opening at the rearmost hoop showed a white landscape, marred only by two lines the wagon wheels had left.

"Your father worked very hard, daughter." Mother sounded stern. "Preparing the lumber which will enable us to acquire a permanent home was not an easy task. Your father is not a well man."

Vienna made no move toward the diary.

"We left our Eastern home so that we can be a family again," Mother continued. "We made a journey of 2,500 miles that taxed our faith in order to be reunited with your father."

Vienna sighed.

"With God's help, our journey is coming to a successful end," Mother concluded.

Vienna felt ashamed. Mother was right. Their journey had been fraught with dangers, but they prevailed. A glance through the rearmost hoop showed long horns coming over the rise. The oxen were safe! Suddenly, Vienna felt wonderful.

Happiness flooded over her as she parted the forward

canvas and looked out past Father, mule, and pony. The wind tore at her hair and rushed in her ears. Through snow flurries, she saw smoke unfurling from a chimney. A sturdy cabin came into view. The cabin sat on the rise, overlooking a flowing creek, stacks of cut lumber, and a millpond.

The prospect of a shelter filled Vienna with unspeakable joy. She closed the canvas against the tearing wind.

"We must thank God for saving us," she answered Mother's questioning look. "If He hadn't sent Pa we'd have perished in the wilderness."

Mother hugged her.

"Whoa!" Father stopped the wagon. "Let's go inside," he called. "We're home for now."